Once again, he kissed her mouth, with searching, bruising lips that were ruthless and demanding. By now he had aroused in her all her instincts to fight against a dreaded Nemesis. She had never known him like this. His savageness was deliberate but, at the same time, Susan recognized something akin almost to desperation in his passion. Without first realizing what it was, a great feeling of pity and remorse welled up in her. It was only now that she knew how deeply he must love her.

"You *will* love me!" he moaned against her mouth. "I can't go on being tormented like this. You're like stone. I need you to be warm and vibrant. I beg you, Sue, my only Sue, love me, love me! I love you so terribly."

THE HOUSE OF ROMANCE # 109
ISBN 0-88933-008-5
Published January 1979

BROKEN VOWS
Copyright © Christine Wilson 1966
First published in Great Britain
by Robert Hale Limited in 1966

THE HOUSE OF ROMANCE is published by
HOUSE OF ROMANCE PUBLICATIONS INC.,
a NEVASCO CORPORATION, Toronto, Canada.

Cover Photo: Colour Library International/
Miller Services, Toronto

Printed in Canada

Trade Mark

BROKEN VOWS

Christine Wilson

House of Romance Publications Inc.

CHAPTER ONE

The string of pearls snapped in Susan Mohr's impatient hands, sending a cascade onto the carpet and under the dressing-table. Tears in her eyes, she watched the rolling gems but made no effort to retrieve them. She blinked rapidly and muttered softly under her breath.

This was just about the last straw!

She was late for the party and still Glyn, her husband, had not come home from the office at his father's enormous factory. Why, oh why had she accepted that invitation for tonight? Glyn had been furious when he found out about it. He was such a bear these days; nothing she did or said seemed to please him. He deliberately went out of his way to upset her, seeming to take some kind of fiendish delight in angering and hurting her.

What a fool she had been to think their marriage could work! Four months of being Mrs. Glyn Mohr, wife of the well-to-do heir to Edward Mohr, owner of a vast network of factories.

Yet she had tried, hadn't she? They had both gone into marriage knowing the difficulties that were besetting them. Why then had they failed so soon and so miserably?

Susan bent down to pick up the pearls. They lay in her palm ... cold and unfriendly. She almost threw them down again in disgust ... that was how she felt, cold and unwanted. At the beginning she had wanted jewellery and all the other many things money could buy. Glyn had promised her everything, yet now none of it held any more interest for her. She knew the broken necklace's worth but all she wanted to do was to throw it away and never see it again.

What was the matter with her? What was she searching for? Why did nothing interest her any longer? What did she want from Glyn?

Susan leant against the dressing-table chair and buried her face in her arm to weep. It was pointless going on. She must make up her mind one way or the other. She had made a terrible mistake. It was useless not to tell Glyn. But when? After the party tonight? He probably wouldn't care if she left him.

The telephone bell shattered the silence.

Slowly Susan rose and went over to the bedside table to lift the receiver.

"Hello, Susan Mohr speaking."

"Sue, it's me," Glyn's voice sounded harsh. "You'd better go without me. I shall be late home and probably unable to make the party at all."

Susan swallowed hard. It had been Glyn himself who had changed his mind so abruptly this morning and said that they ought to go tonight. He was so inconsistent!

"Why couldn't you have told me this morning?" she demanded angrily. "I know your working late is only an excuse. You never wanted to go to Janine's twenty-first party even though she is the daughter of one of your oldest friends. You've telephoned me now just to get pleasure out of knowing that I have gone to a great deal of trouble getting ready."

Glyn's chuckle came over the wire.

"What would you rather do? Enjoy yourself with our friends or dine alone at home with me ... just the two of us ... or does the thought of another dreary, silent evening with your loving husband sicken you?" he demanded fiercely.

Susan bit her lip.

"Glyn. Come home and get ready."

"Why?" the reply was quick and sharp.

"You can't afford to offend any more of your friends, you know."

He laughed bitterly.

"For one moment I thought perhaps you were going to tell me you missed me and wanted me with you."

Susan refused to be goaded.

"Glyn, I don't want to quarrel over the phone. I just want you to take me to Janine's party."

"My dear girl, why should I? Are you afraid of being a wallflower and then no one will dance with you?" he chuckled again. "Surely all your *admirers* will be there? They'll jump at the chance of finding an undisturbed corner in which to have a cosy tête-à-tête with you!" His tone was bantering, then it altered, menacingly. "But remember, my darling, you're *my* wife for now and always, even if you don't behave like one."

Stung by the cruelty in his voice, Susan's reply was quick. How *dare* he say that to her! Heaven knows she'd tried hard enough to hide her dislike of being touched by him, but he had not understood her. Perhaps if she hadn't been quite so seasick during their awful honeymoon ... but all that was past now. Here was the opportunity she had been waiting for. Take it now ...

"Glyn, I'm leaving you."

There was a stunned silence before Susan went on rapidly. "It's no good. We should never have married. After the party I won't be coming back here."

He had found his voice at last.

"Don't be such a little fool! Of course you don't mean it. You're just saying these things to get me home."

"I do mean it!" she declared hysterically. "I can't go on. I'm fed up with your sneering, cruel remarks and the way you treat me ... like ... like a *chattel.*"

"I love you, Susan," he said quietly.

"Pardon?" she had not caught the words.

"Damn it, woman, do I have to shout? I said I love you."

Susan laughed bitterly.

"No you don't. Neither of us loves the other, and that's where we've failed. Now I'm going to ring off. I'm late already. Even if it's the last thing I do for you, I will at least have the courtesy to turn up at the Hobblesons'. When I've gone they won't be able to say I had no manners."

She flung down the receiver. It was done now. Glyn hadn't believed her. Well, she'd soon change all that, she decided grimly, marching to the wardrobe and throwing it open. She tossed her suitcase on the bed and started to cram it full of clothes. She would show Glyn! When he came home tonight the house would be empty and she didn't care ... she didn't care.

Suddenly she began to cry. Long, racking sobs which left her breathless and red-eyed.

Ten minutes later she had backed her car out of the garage and was driving along the road to the hotel she knew to be five miles on the far side of the Hobblesons' large country house. She would book a single room for one night and make up her mind tomorrow where she would eventually go.

As she drove slowly along the winding roads her mind flew back over the past few months, wondering what had driven her to Glyn. Of course it had been That Dress!

The dress had been the star of Maître André's collection and Susan had so longed to be the one chosen to model it. Once again, Maître André had turned her down in favor of Gail. The tall, graceful, willowy Gail whose honey eyes and full smile seemed to win more orders for Maître André than any other model. Susan was very envious of Gail, but in her heart she knew she could never emulate her. Her own figure was excellent but there was something lacking in her poise and manner that she simply could not overcome. Maître André had been kind in his criticism and, although she had not wanted to admit to herself the truth, she knew she would always be one of the "also rans" ... a girl whose face might appear now and again in the top-class journals. No matter how hard she tried, she would not reach the standards she had set herself. If only she could conquer that feeling of lack of self-confidence which plagued her!

Susan watched Gail from behind the alcove. The clever lighting picked out every detail of the dress, sending shadows where the Maître wished them to fall and exposing Gail as an ethereal, beautiful, sylvan creature. Susan's heart sank. She ought never to have chosen modelling as a career!

There was a gasp of admiration from the crowd, then a burst of spontaneous applause. Maître André beamed with delight. Susan watched the audience distastefully. There was the fat, overdressed and over-bejewelled duchess whose body bulged over the sides of her chair like an unset jelly. She ought to be home doing remedial exercises and keeping to a strict diet instead of sitting here wheezing, Susan thought rudely, adding that if *she* had all those jewels she would wear just one or two items at a time so that their full beauty could be enjoyed instead of being swamped by glitter.

Then there was the nervous bride-to-be sitting on the very edge of her chair while her fierce-countenanced mother whispered and prodded her unmercifully. Next to her sat a benevolent old gentleman who always came to the Maître's Occasions although no one seemed to know why. Her eyes passed over the representatives from the British, French and American Press and on to Glyn Mohr who sat in his usual seat at the end of the front row. How he managed to obtain one of the best seats every time the Maître showed a collection, Susan could not imagine, for he was not known as one of the Maître's clients. She thought crossly:

With all that wealth behind him he can buy himself in anywhere!

Earlier today while she had been modelling one of the less exotic gowns, she had allowed herself the luxury of a direct stare at Mr. Mohr and, if there was venom in that fixed smile, then only he had seen it. His firmly closed lips betrayed no secrets and the clear, grey eyes were cool and inexpressive under heavy eyebrows that overhung his face like the thatched roof of a country cottage, thereby giving him an intense, forbidding look. He supported his chin in his clenched hand as the elbow rested on the arm of the chair and, for a moment, the long fingers had uncurled to move very slightly in salutation.

He looks more like the Devil than ever! Susan decided and giggled inwardly. How annoyed he would be to learn that she and the other girls had christened him "Old Lucifer". Of course, that had been before he had spoken to Susan. Even now, when she knew him better, she still could not rid herself of the fitting name.

As she had turned before him, he had caught her eye again and given her a deliberate and broad wink which had annoyed her even more. If she had been standing but a little closer, perhaps she might have endeavored to grind her heel into that elegantly polished toe-cap resting on the floor beyond the crossed legs. The Maître would never have forgiven her for causing an "incident" of almost international proportions during this, his most important collection.

Glyn never seemed to do any work at all! Susan resented this fact. Naturally, he did *have* a job: as one of the directors on the board of the big firm owned by his parents. When he was not making half-hearted attempts at work on the vast premises, he did nothing because, as he had told her months ago, there was absolutely no need for him to work at all. It appeared that no one worried if he did not put in an appearance in the executive offices for weeks on end. He had his father's permission to use his time as he wished.

Until the day five months ago when he had idled into the salon in company with his mother, Glyn had had no purpose in life. Now he was always hanging around the salon, attending every major and minor collection. He was always sitting there ... in the same front seat.

The girls began to wonder about him but not for long. He soon informed Susan why he was there. There were no half-measures with a man like Glyn Mohr, as Susan had swiftly discovered. When he made up his mind to do something, then nothing and nobody stood in his way. From the start his main ambition had been to improve his acquaintance with Susan.

At first she had been a little afraid of the sudden attentions, then she was flattered and intrigued by them. He had lavished money and presents on her, while all the time she was uncomfortably conscious that he was doing so merely to sell himself to her. She had learned quickly that he was a man used to having everything the way *he* wanted it, regardless of whom or what stood in his way.

Naturally Susan had been bowled over by the

promise of riches. She loved being the center of attraction and, after so many years of pinching and scraping, she welcomed Glyn's generosity. He was forceful and persuasive, and liked always to have his own way in the arrangement of the time they spent together. He had every minute planned and she was too busy enjoying herself to question his right of choice. In some way, his being there seemed to make up for her lack of success as a model.

On meeting Edward and Beatrice Mohr, Glyn's parents, the dislike had been mutual. Edward was a man in his late sixties, whose sole occupation and topic was the state of the stock market. Beatrice was an inveterate snob and Susan saw through her within five minutes of their introduction. Unfortunately, Edward had not had the courtesy or kindness to wait until Glyn had taken Susan out of earshot before saying to his blowsy wife:

"Really, Bea, how *could* you allow our boy to take up with that type of girl? Surely there are enough young females among his own set to satisfy him without lowering himself almost to working-class level?

Susan's lips had tightened and she had the pleasure of witnessing Glyn's acute discomfort as he tried to gloss over his father's boorish lack of manners. Yet he need not have worried, for Susan was used to remarks in this vein. After all, over the past years, she had had plenty of practice! She had never quite succeeded in eliminating that slight accent from her speech. It was a legacy from her early days in the working-class area where she had been brought up. Seven years ago, when she had been seventeen, she had won a beauty contest at a holiday camp. It had taken weeks and weeks of hard saving to pay for just one week's holiday away from Mackay's chain store. The prize money and later very fortuitous introductions had been just sufficient to enable her to give up her job as a shop assistant and take up modelling. Admittedly, there had been some very bad days when she had not known where the next meal was coming from, but somehow she had managed: mainly by taking part-time and arduous duties as a waitress in a restaurant. Determination, however, had won, and she had come through safely. If it hadn't been for dear Mum who had contributed a small sum each week ... a sum she could ill afford ... she might have failed.

During the past three years everything had changed. Now it was she, Susan, who was sending home money to help Mum bring up her four brothers and two sisters. The smell of poverty and National Assistance still nauseated her. She had vowed never to be poor again.

Back in the changing-rooms, Susan rested her aching feet. She was dead tired and the thought of bed was enticing. She pushed weary feet into low-heeled shoes, knowing they were not particularly becoming but no one would notice at this late hour. She ran a comb through her unruly hair before cramming it willy-nilly under a saucy hat. Opening her capacious handbag, she thrust all her oddments into it and then prepared to leave the salon.

Now for a hot bath! she thought. Tonight she was too exhausted even to cook herself a meal. Biscuits and cheese and a cup of tea would have to do.

Outside the salon, a sleek grey sports car was drawn up.

How was it that *he* was always able to find a parking space?

She frowned. Tonight of all nights Glyn was waiting. She ought to have guessed he'd be there. If only she'd thought, she could have slipped out of one of the other exits. Hadn't she made it abundantly clear to him only last night that she would *not* be free tonight? But he was a man who would not be denied.

She pulled back sharply, hiding in the shadows, and hoping he had not seen her. With a little bit of good luck, she might be able to slip away in the opposite direction.

However, it was now too late. With the lithe grace of a panther, he had flung open the car door and his huge frame was now striding towards her.

"Where shall we go?" he demanded authoritatively. "I've booked a table at Alberto's, if that's okay with you." It was his choice of place, as usual.

"I'm sorry, Glyn, not tonight, thanks. I thought I'd made that clear yesterday."

"Nonsense! Of course we're going out. You should know me well enough by now, my dear. Hop in!" He pushed her towards the car but she stood firm.

"Glyn, I'm dead beat. I want to go home. Really I do."

For a moment he stared at her, then he scowled, the sardonic devil's eyebrows meeting.

"I want you to come with me!" he protested.

"Oh, for Heaven's sake! Don't you ever think of what *I* want?" she demanded fiercely, and pushed him roughly aside. "If you'll excuse me, I'm off to catch a bus."

"Very well," he said pettishly. "If that's how you

feel, I'll drive you home." Susan looked at him, distrustingly. "I promise," he went on. "First stop your apartment."

He helped her into the car and they drove off.

A sign post loomed ahead and Susan slowed down to read it, then she turned on her left indicator and swung the little car round the tight bend into a side road.

CHAPTER TWO

Susan's lips tightened as she remembered the further events of that evening ... that fateful moment when she had so blindly turned her steps towards this path which was going to lead her straight to a single room at the hotel five miles further on ...

Glyn swiftly negotiated the four miles to Susan's apartment building. It was set back in a quiet side street of unpretentious houses which all bore the sad look of decay. Inside the building there were dark passages and grimy wallpaper, but the two rooms Susan rented were clean and bright. She had purchased a gay material for curtains, and the small knick-knacks she had collected over the past four years served to give the rooms a warm, lived-in appearance. The rent was reasonable, and living here suited Susan admirably, for it meant that her busy mother had one less mouth to feed.

At the front door, Susan turned to thank Glyn for

bringing her home but he was already at her side.

"Key, please," he demanded, and when she began to protest, he went on, "If you won't dine with me, then it's the least you can do to invite me in for a drink," he grinned. "Thanks for saving you your bus fare."

"You know I don't keep spirits!" she snapped. "Not even a beer tucked away anywhere."

He leaned closer.

"Did I say I wanted one, sweetheart? Tea or coffee'll do. Cocoa if you like. They're all nectar from your gentle hands."

The flat was cold and dark, and the meter empty.

"Good thing I came with you," Glyn commented as Susan fumbled in her purse for a shilling.

"I usually leave a couple of shilling pieces beside the meter in case it runs out at an awkward time, which is now. Shillings are in very short supply at the moment. If they don't come and empty this thing, I'll do it myself and blow the electricity company!" she declared, thumping the meter angrily.

Glyn pulled out a handful of silver from his trousers pocket and stood on the landing to hunt through it.

"You're in luck, darling," he said. "Four. These should help for a little while. No. No," he protested quickly as she gave him two florins in exchange.

Susan's eyes sparkled dangerously.

"You'll take these and like it."

"If I refuse?"

"Then it's the last time you take me out, or bring me home."

"Cutting off your pretty little nose to spite your

face, eh?" he enquired lightly, although his eyes were unsmiling.

"Exactly," was her cool reply before she vanished into the kitchenette. "I haven't anything stronger than black coffee, do you mind?"

"I'd rather have white, *if* you can spare the milk," he replied sarcastically. Susan banged a tray onto the table and he grinned, knowing he had annoyed her. Then he joined her in the kitchenette where he leaned against the door jamb, hands in pockets, watching as she filled the kettle before plugging it in. She crossed the floor to the shelf beside him, reaching behind the curtain which cloaked her groceries. He was there before her. Their hands met on the tin of instant coffee. Suddenly he pulled her towards him and stared down at her. Their faces were only a few inches from each other and the air became still. Then, to her great surprise, he raised his hands and gently cupped her face in them, his fingers stroking her cheeks. She had an overwhelming desire to run away ... and one to turn her head until her lips were buried in his palm ... he had never touched her like this before ... their relationship had been so formal and correct ... until now.

Suddenly he released her and went over to the power point to switch on the kettle which she had forgotten.

His back to her, he said steadily:

"Susan, will you marry me?"

He was joking, of course.

"Why?" she asked cheerfully, matching his non-chalance.

"Why do people want to marry each other?" He

turned to face her. His eyes were veiled but he was watching her closely.

"Because ... oh let's stop this silly game!"

"I'm quite serious, Susan. Surely people marry because they're in love with one another, don't they?"

Susan turned from his intent gaze and began to make a great deal of clatter with cups and saucers.

"There's no need to get upset and red-cheeked," he continued, amused. "Surely it can't have escaped your notice that I'm in love with you?" His tone was light and bantering and she was uncertain whether to believe him.

"What do you say?" he added.

She wanted to laugh. Of all the unromantic, brainless ways of making a proposal of marriage! Of course he must be joking. She stared at him and suddenly knew that he was indeed in earnest.

What *could* she say? Glyn was likeable, yes. Naturally he had plenty of faults, but so did everyone else, herself included. He often behaved like a spoiled child but this did not detract from his attractiveness. He was far too free with his money and liked getting his own way. However, he knew her background and even the sordidness of her past had not deterred him; he took her at face value and she enjoyed being pampered by him. No matter where they went or what they did together, she never had the dreaded fear that he was unable to pay for anything. And it wasn't as if she was a success at modelling. It would be irksome to admit defeat but to marry Glyn would be a means of bowing out gracefully.

Yet to love him! That was a completely different matter.

Uncannily, almost as if he was reading her thoughts, he broke in:

"I know damned well that you don't love me, Susan, but you need the things I can give you. Putting me aside for the moment, think of all the dresses, jewels, enjoyment and luxury I can give you once we are married. Everything you've ever wanted can be yours. A decent home, food and warmth, no need to wear yourself out each day at the Maître's. Think of it, Susan, think!"

Susan shuddered. An intense feeling of shame swept over her for he had exactly mirrored her own thoughts.

"You make it sound so horribly mercenary!" she said.

"I mean to be mercenary, darling! Do you think I haven't been wise to what's been going through that quick little brain of yours all these months? Admit it, darling, you wouldn't have looked at a man eleven years your senior if I hadn't had wealth, now, would you?" Susan was crimson with embarrassment. It was all so terribly true!

Glyn laughed gaily.

"Come on, own up! I know I'm no Don Juan, no Romeo to bring a flutter to the heart of every female who sees me. My nose is too big, my face hard and my hair's almost grey already. I don't profess to be the film star lover who will sweep you into his arms in an ecstasy of madness . . . although I *shall* teach you to love me, my girl!" He paused for a moment, then continued: "I also know that many people consider I'm not a particularly pleasant man to know. I'm selfish, I go for what takes my fancy, regardless of those in my way; I'm luxury-loving and I'm afraid I sometimes drink far more than is good for me. On the other hand, I'm just the man for you, although you haven't recognized the fact yet. You need me, my dear. You are struggling for the many things I already have. Let's say I'm Temptation Personified. All you have to do is to accept my proposal, and everything is yours. There'll be no need to wear yourself out at the salon any more and, be honest with yourself, my sweet," he added gently, "you aren't the top model. I'm going to stick my neck out and you can call me all sorts of names for telling you this, but modelling isn't *really* you, is it? A person of your type has either to be tops or nothing, isn't that so? Come on, darling, back out now while you can ... by marrying me."

Susan turned off the kettle, speechless. Glyn could read her like a book!

"Whichever way you look at it, I'm not at all a bad proposition," he added lightly. "You're a lucky girl. I could give you the names of quite a few women who'd be only too pleased to get their thieving little paws on my father's fortune through me. I'm thirty-five, in good health, and have an almost limitless bank balance. Also, I happen to love you."

Never in her life had Susan conjured up dreams of a proposal like Glyn's. It was extraordinarily forth-right, but honest. It occurred to her that she had heard doorstep salesmen explain their wares in similar manner, and, once again, she wanted to giggle shamelessly. However, her conscience got the better of her.

It was all *wrong*! She must put an end to this before

they went too far. Aloud she said:

"It wouldn't be right. You tempt me with offers of wealth, and everyone but a fool knows that money can't buy happiness. I don't love you and I have no wish to marry without love."

He laughed and came over to her. As he put his arms around her reluctant body, he said:

"My sweet, you are so right! I agree, it most definitely wouldn't be fair. However, you seem to be crediting me with very little sense, you know. At my age you don't expect me to be a novice in this game of love, do you? I assure you that in my skilled hands you could soon be taught to love me."

Susan shuddered, suddenly apprehensive.

"And if we fail?" she managed to gasp.

He put a finger on her lips.

"Fail? Don't you know me well enough by now to realize that I *always* succeed in getting what I want? Besides, who are you to talk of failure? Haven't you worked your way up from almost nothing, letting nothing deter you? Come, darling, let's look on our marriage as just another problem to be solved. Problem, or battle if you prefer to think of it that way, and one we shall win together. *You* need feel no guilt. If I'm willing to take the risk, then surely that absolves you? From now on it will be my responsibility.

" *Will* you marry me?"

She pulled away from him and busied herself at the sink, panic-sticken. Part of her wanted to leap at the chance he had offered her yet somehow she had no wish to commit herself so quickly.

"Your parents don't like me," she hedged. "How angry they'll be! You could do far better for yourself, as I'm sure they'll tell you."

Glyn snorted.

"We needn't worry about them. This is *our* affair, not theirs. *I'm* the one to choose who is to become my wife. Enough of this arguing." He laid his hands on her shoulders and turned her towards him. She was drawn into his arms and kissed in a commanding, authorative manner which she found a trifle distasteful, but felt obliged to acquiesce.

Oh yes, Glyn Mohr, you're certainly an expert in this! she thought grimly. The realization both annoyed and disappointed her. His kiss had been so horribly ... what was the expression? ... business-like, that was it ... What had she expected? The earth to open up beneath her feet or something equally melodramatic? He had told her he loved her, but that was obviously not true, not after such routine kissing. There must have been many, many women before her!

Should she accept? She wanted to do so, although she knew it could easily prove to be a hideous mistake. On the other hand, it was not as if she was deliberately deceiving Glyn, because he had recognized the pitfalls already bringing them into the open for them both to see. Therefore if she said "yes" now, it would be equal responsibility if things didn't work as he had hoped.

She must never allow Mum to suspect that she was prepared to marry Glyn merely for his worldly possessions. Put in those words, it sounded terrible. Which, of course, it was. She was disgusted with herself.

Now Glyn had started to kiss her in a different

manner, and the hidden passion frightened her. He was so masterful and possessive and she mustn't allow herself to be dominated. Remember what had happened to poor Mum because she had allowed herself to be ruled and mastered by Father. He had been a useless, conniving, hard and selfish brute, yet somehow ... and this Susan could not bring herself to understand ... Mum had loved Father passionately and had almost broken her heart the day he had been killed through his own carelessness at work. Twelve-year-old Susan had vowed then and there that never, never, as long as she lived, would she allow any man to beat, cajole, bully or dominate her so completely that she could never call her life her own. When she grew up, even if she loved someone to distraction, she would *not* permit herself to be mastered. *She* would dominate the man she married, not he her!

The man she married!

She was beginning to shake in Glyn's hard embrace and a strange whirl of feeling threatened to engulf her. She was suddenly terrified. She pulled her mouth away.

"Stop! Stop! Oh please stop!" she begged, pushing her hands against his chest. His eyes gleamed dangerously.

"You're rough and you're hurting me."

He released her at once and watched her with a glint in his eyes. She bit her lip, thinking of that embrace. If she was to keep her part of the bargain, she must learn to put up with any distastefulness and try to participate, but it wouldn't be easy. She mustn't lose control of herself.

Drawing a big breath, she made up her mind.

"Yes, Glyn, I will marry you, and I promise I'll try to do as you wish."

He grunted with satisfaction and, to her surprise, lit a cigarette. It was exactly as if he had just completed a business deal to the benefit of both parties.

Hardly the reaction she had expected!

The entrance to the hotel loomed ahead of Susan and she drove into the car park. Inside the lobby, the receptionist greeted her with a smile and, within minutes, the bellboy was showing her up to a neat, clean single room. She flung her suitcase onto the stool at the end of the bed and sat down on the soft bedspread. She had done it! She was alone at last and the break had been made. At the party tonight she need say nothing. Glyn's friends would find out all in good time; she wished to do nothing to spoil Janine's great day.

She knew one couple who would shed no tears over the failure of her marriage! Edward and Beatrice Mohr.

CHAPTER THREE

When Glyn's parents were informed of the impending marriage, they were horrified and proceeded at once to tell their son exactly what they thought of the "girl from the back streets". Beatrice felt he was letting the family down badly, having conveniently forgotten her own background as a parlor-maid, while Edward took it upon himself to do everything in his power to dissuade Susan from marrying Glyn.

He did not realize, however, that each meeting with his future daughter-in-law served only to intensify her purpose. She was determined to surprise them all by the success of her marriage to Glyn. Edward Mohr eventually came straight to the point.

"I know your type. You're a scheming little gold-digger. You've tricked my boy into marrying you." His voice was sneering and his eyes snapped as Susan stared coolly back at him. "You aren't in love with my Glyn!" he accused. "You aren't worthy of him."

"I did not trick Glyn!" she retorted angrily, flushing. "We both know exactly what we are doing, Mr. Mohr. Surely you have sufficient trust in your son to give him credit for knowing his own mind? *I* should have thought he was well beyond the age of requiring parental guidance," she finished cuttingly. "I refuse to discuss the matter further. Anything else you have to say should be said to Glyn."

Mr. Mohr quivered with fury and wagged a finger at Susan.

"I warn you here and now, my fine Miss, that if there should ever be any trouble between you and my son, I will do my all to make certain *you* don't go unpunished."

This augurs a good beginning! she thought wryly.

A few days later, Glyn took her by car to pay one of her rare visits to her mother. Mrs. Onsworth was delighted to see them both and it was plain to Susan that she had taken an immediate liking to Glyn.

"Take care of her," she begged him, with tears in her eyes. "Love her well. She's been a good girl and a fine daughter to me."

"I will," Glyn promised, his throat suddenly dry.

Alone with Susan, Mrs. Onsworth accused:

"What are you playing at, child? You're no more in love with him than I am! It's as plain as a pikestaff to me, your mother. To think that a daughter of mine should agree to marry without love! And he so very much in love with you."

Susan looked up, startled.

"Is it so obvious?" she asked.

"Obvious he loves you or that you don't love him? Both. Maybe not everyone sees through eyes like mine. I loved the weak man who was your father with a passion I could not curb and therefore perhaps I notice more than those who haven't suffered. Haven't you thought what you will be doing to him by marrying him without love?" She gripped Susan's arm. "You'll destroy him. Tell him now, before it's too late! Be honest with him."

Susan smiled, bored with the subject.

"Mother, you're fussing. Hasn't it occurred to you that Glyn already knows I don't love him?"

Her mother stared disbelievingly at her.

"Then why is he going on with this ... this masquerade?"

"Don't fuss, Mum! I'm not deceiving Glyn. We both know what to expect from each other."

Mrs. Onsworth was not to be placated. She allowed Susan to see how displeased and disappointed she felt.

"I don't think I want to come to your wedding, dear," she said before they left the house. Susan bit her lip but said nothing. Mum simply did not understand.

Later that night she cried herself to sleep.

Having temporarily got over her objections to the marriage, Mrs. Mohr decided to organize a large, flashy wedding to impress all her important friends. To her added annoyance, Glyn was dead against all flamboyance.

"What will all our influential friends think of us?" she wailed. "The Courtenay-Hamptons, the Arbuthnots, and those sort of people."

"Mother, I couldn't care less! Susan and I are not a peepshow. Besides, aren't you being hypocritical?

You know damned well you're dead set against this wedding. Susan and I have decided we'd like a very quiet one.''

Mrs. Mohr snorted.

"Oh, very well!'' she snapped petulantly. "Have it your own way. You always did, so I don't suppose you'll change your habits at this late age. I only hope your your *wife* will remember her duty to the family name and start producing an heir as soon as possible. You owe it to your father.''

Glyn's mouth quivered with amusement.

"I assure you, Mother, Susan knows exactly what is expected of her.''

"But do you?'' his mother insisted. Glyn looked away.

"Yes, Mother. You and father have set your hearts on my having a son to perpetuate the family name. I promise that Susan won't fail in her duty.''

The days before the wedding were occupied in finding a house on the outskirts of the town. Glyn eventually purchased a large Victorian monstrosity with three floors. Susan stared at it, aghast.

"How can I be expected to keep all these rooms clean and tidy?'' she demanded. "And why do we need such a huge place?''

"We have to entertain, my sweet,'' Glyn soothed. "And I can certainly afford servants.''

"If we can find any!'' Susan retorted.

"That's all being done, so you needn't worry over that problem. Mother is finding them for us.''

Susan bristled.

"Is your mother going to take over our lives?'' she demanded bitterly.

Glyn laughed.

"Certainly not. I decided you need not have the bother of interviewing people, so asked Mother to do it for you."

"What about furniture for this mansion?" she asked.

"Plenty of time for that. I've had some in store for years now. Stuff that was left me by my grandparents. I doubt if we need buy much, except carpets, of course."

Susan turned away, frustrated. So it had all been arranged for her as usual! A Victorian house, drafty and cold, and full of old-fashioned heavy furniture that took ages to dust. She would have liked to live in a new, modern house, complete with all the latest gadgets and simply-designed furniture, but that was not to be. Once again, Glyn hadn't considered it necessary to consult her.

The wedding ceremony took place early one cold autumn morning. There were only four witnesses, all friends of Glyn's. Afterwards, Susan and her new husband left on a cruising honeymoon to the Canary Isles.

From its very beginning, the honeymoon was doomed to failure. As the liner left port, it was met by a cold and fierce westerly wind which steadily increased as the hours passed. Susan and Glyn stood side by side on deck, watching the swiftly vanishing coastline, until the cold and driven spray sent them seeking the warmth of their cabin.

Glyn had booked a first-class suite so that they might enjoy the utmost privacy. As they went down the companionway, the decks were beginning to roll sluggishly. Susan gripped the handrail and gulped hastily.

"Anything wrong, darling?" Glyn murmured in her ear. She tried to pull herself together, and smiled.

"No. No, of course not," came the gay reply.

Inside their suite, she began to remove her coat and scarf. The floor moved ominously beneath her feet, but Glyn seemed oblivious to this. He came over to her and folded his arms around her.

"Sweet!" he murmured. "At last I have you to myself." His lips travelled down her neck and, as he gently unbuttoned her new blouse, he whispered words she could not hear. Then his mouth met hers, hard and demanding, forceful and expert.

The floor moved again, this time more positively. The hum of engines could be heard somewhere in the distant part of the ship. With all her might, Susan thrust Glyn away and sat down hastily on the bed, her face white and drawn.

"Ooh, Glyn, I think I'm going to be sick!" she moaned.

The weather worsened into a force nine gale which kept up for three whole days. Susan cared little what was happening around her for she lay in bed, too ill to know whether it was night or day. The ship's doctor came to visit her often, with remedies for her seasickness, but nothing seemed to make her feel any different.

The liner pitched and tossed its way through angry, boiling seas. Well muffled against the cold and freezing spray, Glyn paraded the empty decks when it was safe to do so, or else haunted the almost empty public rooms. He brooded unhappily, wishing he had chosen to fly instead of taking Susan by sea. The ship's doctor had expressed the opinion that it would not be wise for Susan to travel often by sea as it had made her so desperately ill. Although he could have had his meals served in the suite, out of consideration for his sick wife, Glyn chose to eat in the main dining-room which was almost deserted except for a few stalwarts.

He felt totally alone, and had plenty of time to think as he watched the grey sea leaping across the ship's bows.

The gale died down but it was many days before Susan felt anything near her old self. It was not until they had dropped anchor in a quiet, sunny harbor that she came up on deck for the first time since leaving the English coast. Pale and shaky, she watched the bustling activity with disinterested eyes.

Now that she was better, Glyn began to assert his authority as her husband. She was disinclined for lovemaking, but knew what was expected of her and therefore resigned herself to the inevitable although she still felt slightly unwell. It was far worse than she had ever imagined. Glyn went about the whole thing with a selfish ruthlessness and lack of delicacy that terrified and completely revolted her. She almost screamed when he came towards her.

When at long last it was all over, he would roll away from her and fall asleep, one arm sprawled across her chest like an iron band and the other hanging over the edge of the bed. She looked at him ... at the thick black hairs that crawled across his arms, and shuddered. It seemed to her that no sooner had he started to make love to her than he was asleep while she was left tense and terrified on her side of the bed.

In a very short time she began to dread the familiar overtures and found herself making all kinds of ridiculous excuses to avoid his proximity. She tried never to undress or change when he was in the room as this always aroused his passion.

It isn't as if he's inexperienced, she decided grimly, it's just that he has no thought or consideration for my share in the relationship.

He was a brutal, selfish lover, while she was merely the tool of his satisfaction. Listening to him snoring at her side, bitter tears welled up. He wasn't giving her a chance! Didn't he realize how ill she had been? She wanted to tell him he wasn't helping her, but lacked the courage. He'd probably laugh at her, and that was something she couldn't bear, not at this early stage. She needed gentleness and understanding, but these she realized Glyn was totally unprepared to give.

She hated their intimate moments and naturally it was not long before Glyn noticed. His mouth twisted in an ugly grimace as he pushed her roughly from him. She clutched at the sides of the mattress to save herself from falling out of bed.

"Is it too much to hope you'll make up your mind to do better once the honeymoon's over and we're home?" he sneered as he rose from the bed. "Some honeymoon!"

"Where are you going?" Susan asked anxiously as he began to dress.

"Does it matter so long as you're on your own?" he snarled and slammed from the room.

She cried herself to sleep, after waiting in vain for him to return. Why, oh why couldn't he try to understand her difficulties?

They met next morning at breakfast. He was already seated when she entered their small dining-room.

"Good morning," he said. "I've ordered for you." There was no apology, nothing, and her intention of going to him to put her arms round him with an early morning kiss swiftly died. Right! She'd show him that two could play at that game.

The quarrel remained hovering between them.

In the days left, they walked the decks, joined in the games and dancing, laughing and talking as before, but when they were alone, there was a coolness that had not been there previously. Glyn did not attempt to make love to Susan again, neither did he kiss or hold her. Shyness kept her from him and she was too afraid of rebuff even to slip her hand into his.

The days dragged by and the dreaded return voyage was calm. Susan was not ill although she felt sick the whole time. At last the honeymoon had ended and they were in Glyn's car driving towards their new home. Its bleak and forbidding exterior came into sight as they entered the long, gravelled drive. Susan's heart sank. Would she ever come to like this monstrosity?

CHAPTER FOUR

After the return from their honeymoon, life for Susan became one almost unending stream of parties and entertainment. All Glyn's friends and associates wanted to meet the new Mrs. Mohr and judge her for themselves. After her first initial qualms, Susan soon discovered, to her great surprise, that she was at once a tremendous success with both the men and the women. She was also gratified to learn that one or two of them had seen her picture in the many fashion magazines they ardently scanned at home.

All Glyn's friends were rich and influential and it came as rather a shock to Susan to find that although she was popular with everybody, she had nothing in common with any of them. The women were empty-headed and idle and usually completely bored with their narrow lives. They had servants to do their housework for them, and nannies to cope with their offspring. Everything and everyone seemed so artificial.

To outsiders, the marriage between Glyn and Susan was made to seem idyllic during those first few months, and only the two participants knew the truth. They had agreed to act normally in the company of others, no matter how difficult life at home had proved. Soon people began dropping sly hints about "the patter of tiny feet" ... a phrase which nauseated Susan. There was a warning light in Glyn's eyes as he made a nonchalant reply:

"Plenty of time for that later, eh, darling?" His smile did not reach his eyes and the grip on her arm hurt her. She almost screamed aloud, but managed to look suitably embarrassed, to the delight of the questioners.

Under the bright façade of happiness, fear and resentment lurked. Glyn was impatient and very resentful of his wife's continued passivity and revulsion. On her part, no matter how hard she tried to pretend, she could not get away from the fact that Glyn made love to her solely to please himself. She willed herself to respond with some ardor but felt nothing. There wasn't even a flicker of warmth within her. She shuddered whenever he came near her, and began to dread even the lightest of his kisses, jerking her head away.

One late evening, while she was washing up the dishes, Glyn came into the kitchen.

"Surely those can be left for Mrs. Coombes when she arrives in the morning?" he demanded.

"I like to do them sometimes."

"Nonsense. You'll ruin your hands. Shall I buy a dishwasher instead? They say they're very good." He came behind her as she bent over the sink, caught her shoulders and began to run his mouth up and down her neck. She leapt away as if he had scalded her with boiling water.

"Damn you, woman!" he snarled, baring his teeth. "What the devil's wrong with you? You're cold, damned cold. Haven't you any spark of fire in you at all?" He seized her in hands that bruised and pulled her round to face him. She pushed wildly against him.

"Not now, I'm busy!" she protested, terrified.

"Damn it, I want to kiss you, and you'll like it!" He caught her head between hands that began to squeeze. Then he gripped her hair and pulled her face up to his. Tears of pain came to her eyes but his were hard and merciless as he brought his mouth down on hers, forcing her to cry out. The kiss was insulting, as he had meant it to be. She slapped him hard across the face.

He jerked back, hand to cheek.

"Please, Glyn, leave me alone!" she begged. "I've got a splitting head."

"'I'm busy. I've got a headache,'" he mimicked cruelly. "Isn't there any excuse you haven't used? Were you born without the capacity to love?" he demanded angrily. His eyes fell on a pile of plates. He picked them up carefully one by one and then with a deliberate and vicious sweep of his arm, he flung them against the wall where they shattered noisily.

Susan cried out. Glyn stamped from the room.

"Where are you going?" she called after him.

"Out. Anywhere but here. To people who know how to appreciate me. Then perhaps I'll get blinding drunk, just for a change."

The front door banged and Susan was alone. She

leaned against the draining-board and cried bitterly. What had she done? Why on earth had she agreed to this marriage in the first place?

Glyn was as good as his word. The following morning Susan was frightened to find him dead drunk on the settee, with the room reeking of spirits.

The invitations continued to pour in. Dances, dinner-parties and the theatre, to say nothing of the countless cocktail parties. Susan's popularity with Glyn's men friends was an added bone of contention between them. With smoldering glances, her husband would watch her as she laughed and talked to his friends, but he said nothing, which served to drive Susan further from him. She enjoyed male flattery and flirted outrageously, yet her heart was heavy.

No man can be patient for very long, and Susan's behavior was rewarded by downright rudeness from Glyn, regardless of whom might be listening. She went red with mortification, an experience which gave Glyn a malicious pleasure.

"I say, old chap, take it easy!" one embarrassed young man was forced to blurt out after a particularly cruel and cutting remark Glyn had made concerning his wife. Glyn laughed sarcastically before replying:

"Take no notice of me, Charles. Susan's so much in love with me that she doesn't care what I say about her, do you, sweetheart?" he added, putting an arm around her shoulders affectionately and brushing her forehead with his lips. But his fingernails bit deeply into the upper part of her arm. She managed to keep a charming smile.

It was not long before Susan began to dread parties,

but Glyn insisted on her accompanying him.

"Must show off my beautiful and *loving* wife!" he mocked. "Don't forget, it'll soon be our turn to entertain here." He leaned over her shoulder as she did her hair. "One day, my girl, someone is going to awaken you and show you what you've been missing. I pity the poor man, whoever he may be!" He pulled a lock of hair ungently. "And for heaven's sake put some color on your cheeks to hide those ghastly rings under your eyes. You'll have people asking if you're pregnant," and he laughed bitterly.

Soon the tension could not be ignored by their friends. Pamela Bristow, the young wife of one of Glyn's co-directors, tried to draw Susan out to confide in her. They were alone in the bedroom, powdering their noses when Pamela urged her to unburden herself.

"Please don't thing I'm prying, Sue, but any fool can see something's wrong between you and Glyn. Would you like to tell me about it? Naturally, I'll treat everything you say with the utmost secrecy, and nothing will go any further. But I can't bear to see you and him so miserable. I know Glyn well. He's been spoiled all his life, we know that, but he does love you!" Pamela sat on the bed and watched Susan renew her lipstick.

"I'd hoped people hadn't noticed what was going on," she began feebly.

"Glyn himself makes it so painfully obvious with his uncharitable remarks. So unlike him, too! Sue, it's useless trying to remain blind, isn't it? What's up? It's so soon after your marriage to be hating each other when all the time it's plain you're in love."

Susan replaced the top of her lipstick.

"I was a fool to marry him! We thought it might work out, but we were mistaken. And it's too late now. Oh, Pam, what can I do?" The plea was a cry from the heart. "Glyn's ... well, he's ..." she faltered.

"Yes, Sue, I know what you're trying to say. He's going out of his way to hurt you. And doing so in the most childish way possible ... in public. Poor old Glyn! He was never allowed to grow up properly. That ghastly mother of his mollycoddled him." She looked at Susan shrewdly. "Yet when we met before you two got married, I thought I'd never seen a man so much in love."

"You must have been mistaken," Susan declared coldly.

"Don't be silly, Sue. Of course he loves you, just as much as you love him."

Pamela just doesn't understand! Susan thought sadly.

"Is it the usual old story?" her friend went on gently.

"What are you getting at?"

"Oh, you're so naïve! Bed, and all that."

Susan got up.

"I don't want to discuss it further!" she said huffily, her cheeks crimson. Pamela sighed and slipped her arm through Susan's.

"Why don't you pop down to your quack's and have a little natter with him?" she suggested. "It's surprising what a short chat can do about putting things right."

Susan did not answer. Downstairs, Glyn was

waiting, one hand on the newel post and a drink in the other.

Oh dear, I hope he isn't going to drink too much, Susan thought. She had seen her husband drunk once only and drunkenness terrfied her. Her own father had often come home drunk ... and Mum had always been red-eyed the following morning ...

"Ah!" Glyn said loudly. "Here at last is my adorable little wife. Where have you been all this time? Surely such diminutive noses don't require all that attention?" he came up a few steps to meet her.

"Be quiet, Glyn!" she urged as people stopped talking to listen to the loud exchange of words. But on he went:

"Swopping wifely confidences, no doubt? Has my wife been telling you little anecdotes that can't be told in public?" He laughed scathingly, then pulled Susan's arm and thrust her towards a very surprised looking middle-aged man. "Here, George, you must dance with my darling Susan. She doesn't dance with me because I like to hold her too close and tread on her toes ... in more ways than one," he added under his breath for Susan's ears only. He held his glass high and squinted at it through one half-closed eye. "While I partake of some more of this nectar. I think perhaps I'll get drunk tonight. Susan's scared of drunks, aren't you, darling? Like she's scared of lots of other things." He brushed past Susan and walked to the bar. She remained at the foot of the stairs, tears stinging her eyes so much that she could hardly see George in front of her. He, naturally was acutely embarrassed.

"Forgive me if I don't accept your kind invitation

to dance," she said to him, "but I'm a little tired. I think I'll go home."

Things couldn't go on like this, she decided. Life became worse every day. It was all her own fault. She had made Glyn like this, and now it was up to her to make amends, although she could not help feeling that a man of stronger character might have had the moral strength to surmount the difficulties.

Glyn was weak, weak. She was disappointed. She hadn't wanted to marry a man who would dominate her, yet, on the other hand, she had not wished to have a man who would permit her to grind him into the dust beneath her heel.

What *did* she want?

Glyn did not come home until very late that night, but she was already fast asleep.

When she awoke, he was standing at her bedside, a deep scowl on his face. She sat up, suddenly scared, and pulled the bedclothes tightly around her.

If only he would beg her forgiveness! The apology did not come. Instead he regarded her with anger in his eyes. She felt a flame of fury rise, threatening to choke her.

"A fine performance you gave last night!" she snapped.

"Indeed? And what of your own? You won't have a small drink with me, you refuse to dance with me, and you repel all my amorous advances." He sat down heavily onto the other twin bed and, leaning over, seized her wrist to twist it painfully. "What is it you want? Another man, perhaps, or a bigger allowance?" He released her, tossing her wrist roughly aside. "All right. You can have more money. I'll arrange with the

Bank to increase your personal spending money. I don't care how much extra you want, as long as it makes you content and more pleasant to live with."

She reached for her dressing-gown and pulled it round her.

"I don't want your money! I don't need anything from you except perhaps a little courtesy and kindness once in a while. Oh God, it's all my fault. We've made a hideous mistake. I should never have married you without loving you."

He stood up and stared at her.

"I understand," he said in a slow voice. "We've been married only a few months and already you're tired of it. You hate everything about me, except my money."

"That isn't true!"

"Then what *is* the truth?" He went over to her and held her shoulders. "Do you know what I should do with you? Rip this damned dressing-gown off and toss you onto my bed, there to teach you the meaning of love." He dropped his arms. "But I won't. Somehow sex doesn't seem to matter any more," he went on sadly. "The battle's over, and I've lost. I don't need you physically. Well, does that please you?" He looked up. "Have I taken a dreaded load from your mind?"

That afternoon Susan heard from her bank manager that her allowance had been doubled.

CHAPTER FIVE

Here she was, a week later, sitting on the bed in a hotel when she had been due at a party half an hour ago. Susan stood up and smoothed her dress. Then she opened her suitcase to take out the present she had chosen for Janine.

Most of the guests had already arrived, and many friends called their greetings to Susan.

Pamela bustled up to her, asking:

"Where's Glyn?"

"He couldn't come. Something to do with late work at the office." Pamela nodded understandingly and then a serious-looking young man came up to whisk Susan away for her first dance. As the evening progressed she was conscious of glances in her direction but no one else asked about Glyn.

It was a magnificent party. The entire ground floor had been emptied of furniture and carpets to provide ample room for dancing. One room at the end of the house had been set aside for games and the bar had been set up in the dining-room which opened into the enormous drawing-room. The conservatory doors were also open so that the orchestra could sit there. The plants and tender blooms had been removed earlier that day so there was plenty of space for everyone to dance and enjoy themselves. A marquee stood outside the open french windows of the dining-room and it was here that a running buffet supper was in progress.

Susan was glad that she had come to the party after all. Janine was so pleased to see her, and introduced her to the current boyfriend, a plain, tall and string-bean-like young man with twinkling eyes set under a shock of unruly carroty hair. His name was Frank.

Altogether there were about one hundred and twenty guests present.

Two hours after her arrival, as she was being led laughing and flushed back to her seat in an alcove after a dance, her eye fell on the immaculately dressed figure of her husband. He was at the bar, a drink in his hand. When he saw her, he raised his glass mockingly and then drained it at a gulp.

Heavens! Had he come here to get drunk? she thought wildly.

She wasn't going to take any risks. This was Janine's party. Glyn wasn't to be allowed to spoil it. Whatever his intention, she must try and get him away from the bar.

"Excuse me," she said to her young escort, and hurried towards Glyn. She guessed that he had come here to cause trouble ... she must prevent it at all costs. She passed Pamela on her way. Pam's arm shot out as she hissed in Susan's ear:

"I tried to catch your eye when I saw him arrive, but you've been far too busy enjoying yourself."

Unfortunately, as she had almost reached the bar, Frank stepped in front of her and asked if he could have the next dance with her. She began to refuse, but Glyn said loudly:

"Go ahead, my dear, I can wait. What I have to say isn't important." She hesitated but allowed Frank to lead her onto the floor. Her feet stumbled as she kept looking anxiously back at Glyn who, his glass replenished for the third time, had now turned back to watch her every movement. He grinned mockingly. To her horror, he suddenly thrust his way through the dancers and reached her side.

"Young man, go find a partner your own age," he said rudely and pushed Frank away from Susan. She trembled and Frank had the good sense to leave them without protest. Glyn put his arms round her and pulled her close ... too close.

"Glyn! You're tight!" she accused.

"Wrong again, my sweet. I may have had a few, one too many perhaps, but my mind is as clear as a bell. I want to talk to you and then I'll get drunk afterwards. Will that suit you?" His voice was loud and carried above the music. One or two couples turned to stare at them.

"Shut up, Glyn. Remember where you are!" Susan admonished, then turned round to search for a way out of this seething body of dancers. He noticed her anxiety.

"Scared of me?" he chided. "Come on, I want to talk to you. You've got some explaining to do." He dragged her roughly towards an open french window which led onto a terrace outside, with sloping lawns beyond.

"Now," he said, all banter gone. "When I reached home I noticed you had carried out your silly threat by packing some of your clothes."

"That's correct. I told you over the phone that after this party I wouldn't be going home, and I meant it. Our marriage is finished ... for good."

He gripped her arms.

"You'll be back. You're just trying to goad me into losing my temper."

She sighed.

"Oh, Glyn, Glyn, why can't you recognize the truth when you see it. We *have* to part. There's nothing left for us. There never was anything at the beginning. Open your eyes! See life for what it really is."

"You can't leave me! I won't let you."

She reached up and pried his fingers free.

"Stop it, Glyn, and pull yourself together. You *have* had too much to drink although you don't think so. If there's one thing I loathe, it's a man who can't carry his drink. I'm not going back to your house ... ever. I've arranged everything." She laughed suddenly. "You know, it's really rather amusing. At long last I've actually managed to do something for myself without having to consult you first. I've made up my mind to leave you and it is now a *fait accompli*. Cheer up, you won't miss me. You said you didn't need me any more."

"Need you!" he growled. "My God, woman, if you'd only known the number of nights I've lain awake longing for the slightest indication that you were inviting me into your bed! I can't understand myself because you're now proving to me that you're nothing more than a . . ." and he used a terrible word. She gasped, then he swung back his hand and hit her with the full force of his arm. Her hand flew to her face and she fell back against the parapet. Lithe as a panther he was upon her, lifting her up by the arms and pulling her towards him.

"I won't let you go! I can't bear any more of this hell we've been going through. Sue, Sue, my darling, promise you won't leave me!" he moaned, his mouth on her throat.

Conscious that they could be seen by anyone passing the lighted windows, Susan knew panic.

"I hate you! I hate you!" she hissed and wrenched herself free. She fled from him across the lawn. Where was the drive? She had lost her bearings but if only she could reach the sanctuary of her car she might escape the man behind her.

Glyn was running close on her heels. She was too late to reach the drive. If she could get to that clump of trees and bushes over there perhaps she could still escape him by doubling back through the tree trunks. Hope and fear spurred her on.

She had almost reached sanctuary and was pushing her way past branches that scratched and tore at her, when she heard his quick, gasped breathing. Then his hands were upon her. She choked back a scream, knowing this would bring people out to see what was wrong. His fingers clutched her dress and there was a ripping sound.

"You've torn my frock!" she panted.

"Damn the dress." His hands were around her

throat and he was shaking her. She began to feel faint. He was saying:

"This time you've gone too far. I'll teach you what it means to thwart me. A man can take so much but there always comes a time when he can take no more."

Dimly she heard the sound of music drifting out from the dance room three hundred yards away, then she lost her balance in a whirl of giddiness. Glyn toppled across her and, momentarily winded, she lay gasping for breath. She could see the tree tops etched against the night sky above her head, then they were abruptly blotted out as he bent to kiss her savagely. She tried to protest but the words would not come. His hands moved swiftly and expertly over her as he loosened the torn bodice.

"No, no!" she moaned softly.

"No one will tell *me* when and where I'm to make love to my own wife!" he declared. "Even if I have to half-kill you to make you submit, I *will* make you love me!" His lips travelled down from her throat and she shivered. Raising her hands to push him off, he caught them both in one of his and pinioned them behind her head.

"You flirt and make eyes at all my male friends, yet refuse to undress if I'm in the bedroom. You behave promiscuously with all but me. Now I'll teach you what it is to be made love to by a man who knows your true, scheming little mind."

Once again, he kissed her mouth, with searching, bruising lips that were ruthless and demanding. By now he had aroused in her all her instincts to fight against a dreaded Nemesis. She had never known him like this. His savageness was deliberate but, at the same time, Susan recognized something akin almost to desperation in his passion. Without first realizing what it was, a great feeling of pity and remorse welled up in her. It was only now that she knew how deeply he must love her.

"You *will* love me!" he moaned against her mouth. "I can't go on being tormented like this. You're like stone. I need you to be warm and vibrant. I beg you, Sue, my only Sue, love me, love me! I love you so terribly."

Suddenly she wanted to accept him, wanted to give in to him, wanted him to dominate. She was tired of fighting on her own in the world. It was a woman's need to be loved and ruled by her husband. Here was a destiny far more powerful than any of the mental barriers she had so carefully erected around herself since her father had died. Glyn was too strong for her ... and all at once she was glad ... terribly glad. She wanted him to have his own way. There was something so different about him tonight. For the first time he needed to arouse her rather than gratify himself. A tide of wild emotion almost drowned her with its intensity. She cried out and pulled her arms away from his grasp. He paused, looking down at her in the dim light.

"I want to love you," she whispered and threw her arms round his neck pulling his face down to her. For a moment he stared down at her in disbelief, then he saw her gentle smile, which told him all he longed to know.

"I love you, Sue," he whispered.

She stopped fighting him and matched his passion

with her own. She was being carried along on great waves of glory. She wondered if she could bear it. Then the world shattered into a thousand pieces.

"All hate gone?" she whispered eons later. He raised himself on one elbow and gently stroked the cheek he had hit back there on the parapet.

"Forgive me, darling, forgive," and touched her lips with his. The kiss was gentle and suppliant.

The party was still in full swing when Susan and Glyn crept towards the drive. Glyn opened the car door.

"Don't you think I ought to drive?" Susan asked, as Glyn stumbled slightly.

"My dearest wife, I haven't had all that many drinks!" he protested. "I think I'm quite capable of driving you home in my own car."

"We could take mine," she urged, but Glyn was adamant. He got into the driver's seat but before he turned the ignition key he put his hand over hers and asked:

"You will come home with me?"

She nodded, astonished and delighted by the warmth of love she now felt for him.

"Please, if you still want me."

He laughed joyously. The car seemed to sway dangerously across the road as they left the large country house. Neither noticed nor worried. All Susan could think of was the exciting realization that she loved Glyn after all. Whatever had held her back in the past, its fear had gone like a puff of wind. They had their whole future before them, and she meant to make the most of it. There was so much to be said, but it could all wait until they reached home. The memory of tonight in the garden was too close, too poignant.

She stretched out a hand to touch his as it lay on the steering-wheel. His hand was so strong and no longer frightening in the light from the dashboard. In reply, he turned to look down at her.

Too late she realized what she had done. Too late she saw the sharp corner. In diverting his attention he had allowed the car to swing across the road. His reactions must have been slowed by the whisky he had drunk earlier, and he was unable to correct the swerve. The corner flew to meet them, Glyn fighting for control. The engine howled madly as the car crashed into a tree.

CHAPTER SIX

At first Susan could not understand what was wrong. There were people moving about her, as if in a haze, and dim voices were speaking:

"Careful now, take her away while we try to get the other free ... badly injured ... where's that doctor with the morphia?" Then there was oblivion.

Hours later she opened her eyes. The ceiling above her head was white and it met a wall in which there was a door. Her eyes travelled past this door seeing the blood-drip stand and restfully patterned curtains suspended over the bed in which she lay. Many pillows kept her in a semi-recumbent position. She lowered her eyes and started. Both her arms were encased in bandages, and she realized that to draw a breath was an effort causing pain. She tried to move, but the ache in her head and chest soon stopped her.

Suddenly there was a nurse at her side.

"Where did you come from?" Susan asked, her mind bleary. The nurse smiled.

"I've been here all the time, Mrs. Mohr," she patted the bedclothes and felt the pulse in Susan's neck. "You must lie still. Are you feeling a little more comfortable now?"

"Where am I?" Susan whispered.

"In a private room of St. Stephen's Hospital."

"What ... what happened?" The drugs were preventing her from coherent thought.

"You were involved in a car accident just before midnight last night."

"What time is it now?"

"Almost five in the morning. Now you must go to sleep again."

Susan turned her head to the window where the early morning light was beginning to illuminate the world outside. Birds were singing gaily.

"Why are my hands like this?" she said disinterestedly.

"They were badly cut. The doctor said there was no need to worry as they'll heal very quickly. He'll be in to see you later today. Now, dear, try to drink some of this." She turned away to pick up a feeding cup which she held to her patient's lips.

Memory suddenly came flooding back, and Susan jerked herself up in bed, only to fall back in acute pain.

"Glyn!" she moaned. "My husband, how is he? Is he hurt too?" She had remembered now. It had been he who was driving. Then there was that dreadful bend and the terrifying swerve and that was all.

The nurse eased Susan back onto the pillows and held the cup for her. She said in a matter-of-fact voice:

"Your husband's in a room further along the corridor. He's also been hurt, but Doctor can tell you more about him, later."

Fear gripped Susan.

"He isn't ...?"

"Of course not, Mrs. Mohr! Like you, he needs as much rest as possible. Now you really must sleep."

Surprisingly, Susan fell asleep almost at once. When she re-awoke she discovered that it was almost two o'clock in the afternoon. The room was bright with the early May sunshine which helped her to feel very much better. Her head ached only slightly now but she was stiff all over. When the nurse came to tidy her bed, Susan asked for a mirror.

"I expect I look awful!" she said, smiling ruefully. "Am I in for a shock?" The nurse opened a drawer and withdrew a hand mirror which she held up in front of Susan's face.

"There, Mrs. Mohr. Believe me, it isn't all that bad."

Susan gasped.

"Oh!" A vivid bruise disfigured one cheek and the other was showing the beginnings of a magnificent black eye.

"I expect you banged your head against the dashboard," the nurse suggested. "It almost always happens. But don't worry. By the time you're allowed to leave, most of the bruising will have faded. It always looks far worse than it is for the first day or two."

Susan bit her lip. She knew what had caused the mark across her cheek. She had been too scared to realize at the time how hard Glyn had hit her.

"I'd like to see my husband." The nurse placed the mirror on the bed-table.

"Sister can tell you more than I. I'll let her know you're awake," and she hurried away, leaving Susan to lean her head back against the pillows. In the distance she could hear the bustle of the hospital and busy traffic somewhere a long way from the building.

A few minutes later Sister came into the room. She was a small woman, dressed in dark blue, with snow-white cuffs and a dainty lace cap on her head. She looked very young for such responsibility. At her side walked a stout, middle-aged man whom Susan rightly took to be the specialist. He looked her over thoughtfully, picked up the chart from the table near the door and then came over to her.

"You're feeling better? Good." His voice was gruff but kind. He leaned over her looking into each eye in turn.

"Headache almost gone?" Susan nodded. "Hands comfortable?"

He motioned to Sister who leaned over to undo Susan's pajama jacket. It was an ugly article belonging to the hospital and its wearer vowed to have her own clothes brought to the hospital as soon as possible. The specialist examined the strapping that had been put round Susan's chest and then stood back while Sister rearranged the clothes.

"Now, Mrs. Mohr, you've had a slight knock on the head, but I doubt if the skull is fractured. Just to make certain, I will arrange for the portable X-ray unit to visit. At the same time I'll want your ribs re-X-rayed. There are three cracked ones which should mend in no time, and a few deep cuts and grazes on your hands and arms. Otherwise I think you'll live." He smiled engagingly down at her.

"A couple of weeks in bed here and then you'll be able to go home. However, we'll review that some time next week."

"Please, Doctor, how's my husband?" she begged anxiously. The doctor scratched his chin thoughtfully.

"Ah, yes, Mr. Mohr. Now, Madam, I'm not going to beat about the bush. You'll be wanting the truth, naturally. Your husband's injuries are very much more serious than your own. I understand he was driving?"

"Yes."

"His left leg is fractured in three places, and we've put it in traction. You know what I mean?" Susan understood.

"Later, when his general condition improves we'll attend to the fractures more thoroughly, but at the present time any operation is inadvisable. He had a very bad knock on the head, fracturing his skull in two places; fortunately, without depression. He's still deeply unconscious and all we can do is to wait until he comes round." He patted her bandaged hand soothingly.

"You mustn't fret, Mrs. Mohr. A lapse into unconsciousness is Nature's sole way of giving the brain the rest it so badly needs after damage has been suffered. There's nothing at all unusual in a patient remaining unconscious for hours, sometimes days, following a serious road accident."

"I must see him!" Susan declared frantically.

"My dear, it'll do neither of you any good. When

he's come round, then we'll see if you can visit him, but for the time being it's better for you to stay in bed.''

''Couldn't I just see how he is? Even if he doesn't know me, I don't mind as long as I can see him.''

''No, Mrs. Mohr. You're far from well yourself, and it will only aggravate your own discomfort to allow you to move about too soon. Tomorrow? Well, we'll see how you are in the morning.'' He smiled again and turned to Sister.

''If there's anything you need, Sister can get it for you. Goodbye for now, Mrs. Mohr, and sleep all you can,'' and the two of them left the room.

Two minutes later, the Sister came back.

''Mrs. Mohr, I'm sure you'd like some of your own things. If you care to give me a list and the name of someone in your house, I can arrange for them to be brought over here. Also, things for your husband.''

Susan bit her lip.

''I . . . I have a room at the Three Cross Ways hotel, it's number fifteen, I think. My suitcase is there already. Perhaps you'd better contact my husband's parents to bring his personal belongings,'' she suggested, after a pause. ''They'll have to be told about Glyn as soon as possible. Do you mind?'' she looked helplessly at Sister who did not betray her surprise by a flicker of an eyelid. No doubt, thought Susan, she was used to coping with awkward situations. She hoped Mr. and Mrs. Mohr would not ask to see her. She couldn't face them today. They'd be sure to blame her for the accident.

Less than two hours later, she heard the familiar tones of her father-in-law raised in anger just outside the door. Then the soft ones of Sister's, soothing and placating. Then the talking died away as footsteps receded. Susan was almost asleep again when the door opened and Sister said:

"Mr. Mohr would like to see you."

"No!" But it was too late. Edward marched into the room. He stopped at the foot of her bed, staring down at her, dislike and suspicion on his face.

"Well, what have you to say about all this?" he demanded. "What have you and my boy been doing to get the car and yourselves into such a mess?"

Susan explained as well as she was able. She told her father-in-law how they had left the party, and about the car swerving off the road.

"Have you seen Glyn?" he snapped. Susan shook her head.

"I'm not allowed to get out of bed yet."

"Well, I've seen him, and he looks terrible," Edward announced bluntly. "I insisted on seeing him."

At that moment there was a knock at the door and a junior nurse came in. She carried Susan's suitcase.

"The hotel has just sent this over, Mrs. Mohr. I'll come back later to unpack for you." She put it in a corner of the room and then hurried out. There was silence.

"Hotel? What hotel? What was she talking about?" Edward demanded. "Glyn didn't say anything about the two of you going away. Besides, I brought his things. Why weren't they with yours?"

Susan leaned back and sighed.

"Does it matter?" she murmured wearily.

"Not at the moment. I'll wait for Glyn to explain."

He moved over to the window and looked out. "I suppose the young fool had had too much to drink at the party."

"No more than anyone else," Susan said.

"Of course he did!" Edward came towards her and wagged his finger at her menacingly. "Until you came into my son's life, he never once over-indulged, but since you two married, at times he's had just a few too many. Oh, don't bother to deny it! Word gets around, you know. You can't keep juicy bits of gossip like that hidden for long. Some people delight in telling those who are nearest and dearest! I was one of the very first to hear about my son's shortcomings, never fear."

"He's only been drunk once!" Susan protested wearily.

"Nonsense! I've heard about the things he says to you in public. If that isn't alcohol in his veins, then what is it, eh? I brought my boy up with good manners and breeding. Of course it's too much drink that's been loosening his tongue! And I blame you."

Susan turned her head into the pillow. How could she possibly explain to ... to this dreadful man the real reason for his son's behavior? It *had* been partly her fault he had treated her so cruelly, but he wasn't a drunkard!

"It was *your* fault Glyn was drunk last night!" his father accused bitingly. "Your fault he crashed the car and almost killed himself."

"Please go away!" Susan had begun to cry. "Leave me alone. My head's hurting."

"You may cry now, my girl, but if our Glyn has to suffer because of you, then this won't be the last you'll hear of it. Not by a long chalk!"

With that Edward Mohr stamped from the room.

Susan fumbled blindly for the bell-push pinned within reach of her counterpane. A scared-faced nurse took one look at the sobbing patient and rushed away to fetch Sister. Sister soothed and comforted with words as she prepared a sedative.

"I don't want Mr. Mohr ever to come in here again!" Susan wept. "Please, Sister, I can't bear it!"

"I'll see that he doesn't upset you again, Mrs. Mohr. Now please calm down. We can't have visitors upsetting our patients like this, can we?"

Susan spent a troubled and restless night. Edward haunted her in her dreams, forever pointing his long, accusing finger at her as he leaned over the limp body of his son.

The following afternoon, Susan was allowed to see Glyn. Two nurses helped her into a wheelchair. It was quite an effort to move, but she managed it, protesting only slightly. Then she was wheeled along the corridor towards the room where Glyn lay. Outside the door a notice proclaimed:

"Quiet please. Absolutely no visitors without
Sister's permission."

Inside the room, Glyn lay with closed eyes in a bed similar to the one Susan had just left. The blinds were down, shading the room. His left leg was supported in a cradle and traction ropes and weights overhung the foot of the bed. A blood-and saline-drip stood at the left-hand side of the bed, while a nurse sat quietly on the right-hand side, watching the patient.

Susan was wheeled over to that side of the bed, the nurse rising to make room for her. She looked down at her unconscious husband. His head was bandaged, one eye badly swollen and bruised, while almost his entire face was covered with cuts and scratches. His hands lay white and still outside the bedclothes.

"Glyn!" she whispered. The nurse bent over her.

"He can't hear you, Mrs. Mohr. He's still deeply unconscious."

Susan wanted to cradle one of those limp hands to her lips but her own were awkward and unwieldy, so she had to content herself with staring at him.

"Has he been like this all the time?" she asked the nurse. "I mean, ever since the accident?"

The nurse nodded.

Susan was allowed to stay for five minutes, after which she was wheeled back to her own room. She felt lonely and strangely depressed, longing only for Glyn to regain consciousness.

CHAPTER SEVEN

Susan was obliged to go through the formality of an interview with the local police regarding what she could remember of the accident. Sister had refused to allow the police sergeant to talk to Susan for two days but in the end her patient felt well enough to make her statement. Reluctantly she had to admit that they had been to a party but was emphatic that Glyn had not had too much to drink.

"There was a witness to the accident, Mrs. Mohr," the sergeant went on kindly. "He was coming out of a side turning and saw your car take the corner too widely and collide with that tree. He has made a full statement and, if it's any comfort to you, he doesn't consider the car to have been driven recklessly. There may be a case of driving without due care or control but I hope not one of driving under the influence of drink. You must realize that the hospital authorities say your husband was smelling quite strongly of spirits when admitted."

"But he hadn't had too many, officer!" Susan protested.

"I hope to be able to interview Mr. Mohr for myself when he's better, although, of course, I don't expect him to remember very much after head injuries and being unconscious so long." He put away his notebook. "We shall rely on the witness, and possibly your own testimony." He smiled as he rose to leave. "But you needn't worry, Madam, no steps can be taken until your husband is well enough to attend court."

He left Susan with plenty to think about. She had not known that those with head injuries often forgot what had happened. How much was Glyn to forget? she wondered, and made up her mind to ask the House Surgeon.

When he visited her that evening, and she put her question to him, he replied:

"Yes, Mrs. Mohr, it's usually the case with head injuries and concussion. A state of what we term 'retrograde amnesia' occurs. This means that the patient can forget some of the events leading up to the actual injury. For instance, in slighter cases, such as that of a child falling out of a tree and bumping its head, he may not even remember climbing up in the first place, let alone tumbling off a branch! The more serious the brain damage, the longer the period of amnesia." He looked down at his hands. "It may be possible that when Mr. Mohr eventually wakes, he may not remember leaving the party or even going to it!"

Susan frowned.

"My father-in-law thinks Glyn had been drinking

heavily, but he'd only had a few, doctor. Will that make any difference?"

"Depending on how well he can tolerate spirits, his memory might have been a little blurred already, which will put our time back even further." He looked at her. "Does it matter, Mrs. Mohr? Wouldn't it be better for him to remember little about the evening?" His suggestion was gentle and sympathetic.

"He *wasn't* drunk!" Susan cried aloud. "But no one will take my word. Oh, everything's so horribly muddled, I just don't know what to think!"

When she was on her own again, the problem whirled round and round her mind. It was possible that Glyn would not even remember how they had fought, and the eventual, wonderful reconciliation. Hot blushes swept over her as she thought of that evening. Perhaps he might even have forgotten that she had threatened to leave him? If Glyn could remember only that they were living together under difficult conditions, forgetting the reconciliation and all that had led up to it, then she would have to act cautiously. Her spirits rose. When they were both home again, she could make it up to him! Especially if he had forgotten her threat to leave him.

The suitcase from the hotel! How could she explain that? Edward Mohr was certain to ask Glyn about it. Oh, No! She must stop him, but how? To raise the matter again was tantamount to arousing fresh suspicions in her father-in-law's mind. Better left alone and hope for the best.

If Glyn should ask her about the party, what then? She could not tell him the truth . . . it was too personal and poignant.

He ought to know, a small voice prompted her. Yet if she told him, he'd probably sneer at her, accusing her of pure invention and she did not think she would be able to face his scorn and derision quite yet.

It was not until five days after the accident that Glyn regained consciousness. Susan was wheeled in to see him again. The nurse placed the wheelchair at his side and left them alone. Her heart thudding painfully, Susan looked at her husband. His eyes were closed and he was lying very quietly in bed.

"Glyn!" she whispered and gently laid her hand on his. With a shudder he pulled his away, turning his head towards her and opening his eyes. Then he shut them again as if he was in great pain.

"Go away!" he whispered, then raised his voice. "Nurse? Nurse! Where are you?" Immediately the door opened and the nurse bustled in again.

"I'm here, Mr. Mohr. Is there anything you want?"

"Take my wife away. I don't want to see her. I've nothing to say to her and am certain she has little to say to me." His voice was hard and cold.

"Glyn, darling, I must talk to you!" Susan begged, tears welling up. She reached for his hand again but he jerked it away from her. "Why don't you want me with you?"

Glyn turned to look her full in the face.

"Don't hedge. I'm not dying, you know. You were leaving me and my head's aching far too much for me to argue about it now."

"No, Glyn! I'm not leaving you!" she protested.

"Why not? Because I've hurt myself?" He laughed, a hollow, mirthless sound in the back of his throat. "Don't be such a fool, Susan. I don't need you. Especially not now. It was all over before we crashed. Finished. Weeks and weeks ago. We can't use the accident as an excuse to carry on the ridiculous farce of the last months."

"Please, Glyn. I can make it up to you, I promise."

"Make it up? Why? Can't you get it into that pretty little head that I don't need you now? And for goodness' sake, stop snivelling, woman!" He put his hand to his head and went on: "I've forgotten what happened that evening except that you told me you were leaving me, and I saw some of your clothes and hair brushes had gone. I remember that all right. It was the first thing I knew when I woke up today."

"It wasn't true!" Susan cried.

"Don't lie to me, sweetheart. You know damned well we can't live together. Shall I tell you something, my poor pathetic little wife? The first thing I realized when I came to was that I felt glad and strangely at peace with myself and the world. Do you know why I had that feeling? It was because my problem had been resolved. You and I were finished and I was glad ... glad."

CHAPTER EIGHT

Susan was almost hysterical when she reached the privacy of her room, and Sister sent for the House Surgeon. A sedative having been prescribed and given, Susan lay back in bed, waiting for sleep to drown her unhappiness.

Glyn had forgotten everything but their bitter words, and her threat to leave him. The events of the party and afterwards were as if they had never been. As far as he was concerned, their married life was over, and he was profoundly glad. But she could not allow it to be so!

A small ray of hope shone forth. He was still very unwell. Later, perhaps, when they had both been discharged from hospital and were at home again, she could bring him to realize that it *was* possible for them to live together. In another day or two, when he had regained more of his lost strength, he would be a different man.

Susan was too optimistic. In the meantime, Glyn's

father had visited his son and told him everything, including Susan's hotel room. He had even gone so far as to check the register for himself for absolute proof. When Susan was wheeled into Glyn's room, he waved her away again.

"I refuse to continue quarrelling with you. My father has confirmed everything I wanted to be sure of. Nurse, Mrs. Mohr won't be staying. Please take her back to her room."

Later, from the gossip Susan picked up from the nurses, she learned that Glyn had insisted on being moved to a room on a lower corridor, to be away from her. The nursing staff seemed to know what had happened and Susan found their compassion almost too much to bear. No doubt they discussed both herself and Glyn at great length behind her back, but she did not care.

The specialist told her quite calmly and kindly that he was afraid he was unable to permit her to visit her husband, as he had threatened to discharge himself unless his request to refuse Susan access to his room was carried out. Reluctantly, the medical staff had agreed to concede. Susan, however, was not placated by the specialist's explanation that Glyn needed rest and quiet and on no account was he to be upset or excited.

All through her illness, Susan had received many gifts of flowers and fruit from Glyn's friends and their wives, but she refused to see anyone. Not even Pamela.

Edward and Beatrice sent her nothing, although she had one further visit from the former.

"My son has told me everything," he began. "It's

just as I expected. I knew this marriage was a dreadful mistake, and I've been proved right. He has told my wife and I that you had left him and we all agree that it was the best thing you have ever done."

"I'm not leaving him now!" Susan protested hotly.

"Oh? Changed your mind? Why? Are you afraid you won't be able to get your greedy little paws on Glyn's money?"

"How *dare* you!" Susan was quivering with fury. "I don't want money. I want Glyn."

"Unfortunately for you, my dear, he doesn't want you," her father-in-law snapped viciously. "He and I have discussed what must be done. He has to remain in bed for many weeks yet, but, with my wife's help and that of a trained nurse, we've arranged for him to be cared for at our house. He'll be given expert care and attention ... also love, a commodity which you have proved sadly incapable of giving," he added harshly. "The front door will be barred to you, Susan, at Glyn's personal request. The Mohrs don't want you. Have I made myself quite clear?"

"Perfectly," Susan replied, with the light of battle in her eyes. "But I'm warning you all, don't expect me to give up Glyn just because you've ordered me to do so, because I won't. Glyn's my husband, and I mean to keep him, whatever you say."

Edward Mohr laughed softly.

"Oh, my dear girl, how foolish you are!" he said and then left the room. The laugh and the pity in it frightened Susan far more than the threats and scorn.

Three days later she was discharged from hospital and returned to the bleak house she knew as home. It stood dark, dreary and impersonal, and suddenly she hated it with an intense loathing. It had never been what she could call a proper home, and neither of them had tried to make it one. Even their own personal effects around the place looked awkward and out of character.

Susan knew that Glyn was being transferred to his parents' home in four or five weeks time, despite Edward Mohr's assurance that it was to be sooner ... Glyn had needed further operations on his fractured left leg, and the medical staff in charge of his case advised him to remain under their care until these operations had been completed.

During this time Susan did not visit the hospital, although she wanted to very much. Instead, she stayed at home, reading and watching television, but the place was quiet and tomb-like. She had no inclination to go out and enjoy herself, but Pamela called on her regularly, bringing her magazines and the latest tidbits of gossip. Unfortunately, it seemed to Susan that the whole world knew about her parting with Glyn. Pamela's sympathy was almost too much to bear. Susan remained listless and disinterested. Her doctor prescribed a tonic to buck her up but she was not to be enlivened.

Somehow the weeks passed. She rang the hospital and learned that Glyn was being discharged the following day. Immediately she put on her hat and coat and rang for a taxi to take her to St. Stephen's.

She found Glyn sitting by the window of his room, his left leg encased in a plaster and propped up on a stool. He turned to look at her with a complete lack of emotion, and her heart sank. She came to stand beside him and noticed for the first time that his hair had become more grey during the seven weeks he had been in hospital. The sunlight danced on it and she longed to run her fingers through it.

"Glyn, I've come here today to beg you to change your mind and come home with me tomorrow," she began shakily.

"Your place is with me. I can give you the care and attention you need." He shook his head.

"No, Susan, that part of my life has finished. I've made all the necessary arrangements with my parents. I'm far too tired and disinterested to live and quarrel with you."

"But we needn't quarrel! Not any more," she protested, reaching for one of his hands. He removed it slowly and stared up at her.

"No, Susan, it's too late. Our marriage has died; long, long ago. Almost before it began," he added sadly.

"Glyn, do you remember anything at all that happened the night of the accident?" she urged but he shook his head.

"Very little. A few days previously you and I had quarrelled bitterly, then the evening of the party I rang up to tell you I wouldn't be going. You then said you'd leave me. I was furiously angry and decided to go to Janine's after all. When I got home to change, you'd already left, complete with packed bag, bound for some hotel or other, I presumed. I am told, however, that when I got to the party, we had some sort of scene. Father says I possibly drank too much because I was so angry with you. True?"

"Yes and no. We argued just like all the other times in public except ..."

"Don't bother to go on," Glyn interrupted. "I can well imagine what happened afterwards. We went on quarrelling; there's no need to deny it because everybody knows we left the place busy arguing. Everyone knows everything ... except me, of course," he added bitterly.

Clutching desperately at a straw, Susan cried:

"They don't know *everything*!"

"My friends have tried to make light of it, but I must have behaved abominably, only they're too good natured to admit it. Because I was tight ..."

"You weren't."

"I must have been. Why else should I drive into that confounded tree?"

"Glyn, if we were quarrelling, haven't you wondered why we were both in your car?" Susan pressed urgently, reaching for the opening he had given her.

Her husband shrugged his shoulders disinterestedly.

"I can't imagine, and I don't particularly care now. We were in my car which hit a tree. That's all there is to it."

Susan turned away! He was in one of his stubborn moods when she knew he certainly wouldn't listen to her.

"Can't we start afresh?" she whispered. "Please, Glyn? Give me just one more chance!" She sank onto her knees beside his chair and looked up at him beseechingly. His eyes were scornful.

"For heaven's sake, get up, Susan! I loathe people who come crawling to me. There's absolutely no need to indulge in these histrionics. I'm too weak and tired to make the effort to start afresh now. All I want is to be allowed to live in peace and quiet without the eternal bickering and tension. We never had anything in common after all, did we? You were right. We shouldn't have married. It was then that I had the misfortune to be in love with you ... no, don't interrupt ... but now even that has disappeared." His face was pitying. "What's left?"

Susan rose and went to the window so he should not see her grief.

"I was foolish, Susan. I'd hoped you'd come to love me when all the time I was so blind I couldn't see it was only the glitter of wealth you loved."

"Glyn, you're wrong, so very wrong! It's *you* I love!" she protested in a choked voice.

"Bah! Funny way you have of showing it, my dear! At the moment all you feel for me is pity because I've been injured physically. I'm an invalid who needs careful attention, and you pride yourself on being the one most suited to the task." He turned sharply in his chair and raised his voice. "I don't want you or your pity. I want to be left alone, understand?"

"Don't you care at all what I do?" she asked going to his side.

"As we're being frank with each other this afternoon, then I'll give you a frank answer. No. I'm beyond both love and hate. I'm just completely disinterested. Oh, I'll see you're well provided for and want for nothing financially, never fear."

She leaned over him, her eyes snapping.

"I know who's behind all this! Your father's been at work. He's talked you into 'buying me off'. Well, you tell him this, Glyn Mohr, I wouldn't touch a penny of your filthy conscience money, not even to save me from starving. I'd rather steal than accept money from you or him!'' She marched to the door where she paused to fling back at him:

"I wish you joy while living with your parents. I've heard of women running back to Mother, but never of a man!'' and she slammed the door hard.

CHAPTER NINE

Susan toyed with the idea of going to see her mother, whom she had not visited since before her marriage. She had meant to see her soon after their return from the honeymoon but as life with Glyn had not started smoothly, she had decided to put it off until things were a little happier between herself and her husband. As the time passed, she had become more apprehensive. Her mother's disapproval of the intention to marry a man she didn't love had shamed her deeply and she had not dared to admit how true her mother's prophecy had proved. Now that the marriage was over, she found she could not take the step. Kinder to let her remain ignorant of the truth, Susan decided. Fortunately there had not been very much publicity given by the newspapers to the accident. Now, if she had been an ex-top model, how they might have splashed it across their pages!

As far as Mrs. Onsworth was concerned, the less she knew the better.

Susan had a far more important and immediate problem to consider now. What was she to do? To continue living in this mausoleum was entirely out of the question. She must find a small apartment, and perhaps the Maître would give her back her old job. There were great doubts about that, however, because there were plenty of other models of her standard. Still, she'd try, but not today. She did not feel up to making the effort of calling on her former employer, and the rigors of modelling were a little too much to consider at the present time.

She had not felt at all well since the accident. She was listless and tired easily, probably all due to having fractured her ribs, she decided. And her back had begun to ache almost incessantly. By the end of a morning she was quite glad to lie on the settee and sleep. Idly, she looked at herself in the long mirror beside the dressing-table.

Mm! she thought ruefully. Some strict dieting needed here if she was to resume modelling. Too much flesh had been added since her marriage, especially around the hips. Before she even asked the Maître to take her back, she would have to start getting rid of this excess.

Two days after Glyn left hospital, the weather became abominably hot, making Susan feel very ill. She was giddy with the heat, and food nauseated her. The first afternoon she felt unwell, she put herself to bed in a darkened room where she slept fitfully. After a restful night, she arose feeling more like her old self again, yet halfway through breakfast she had to push the food away and dash wildly for the bathroom. White and shaken, she emerged a quarter of an hour later. Obviously she must have eaten something that had gone off in the heat, because hot summer days had never afflicted her in this manner.

When the same thing happened again on the next two mornings, she was obliged to sit down on her bed and think carefully. A great suspicion had grown in her mind. This was no food-poisoning! She stared at Glyn's empty bed and the more she thought about it, the more it seemed possible.

How many weeks since the accident? Eight? Nearly nine? One by one the little pieces of jigsaw slipped into place. Of course! The listlessness and backache and general feeling of *malaise* that she had put down to the after-effects of the car smash. She rose and looked at herself in the mirror. Yes, the thickening around the hips . . . she was going to have Glyn's baby!

Her flushed and excited face stared back at her. How thrilled Glyn would be to learn the truth! She knew he had always wanted a son, and the elder Mohrs had made no pretence of their eagerness for a grandson to carry on the family name. Now that there was a baby on the way, Glyn would forgive her for everything that had happened and they would make a fresh start together.

A sudden doubt assailed her.

Could she tell him the truth? He might not believe her. After all, why should he? As far as he knew there wasn't the slightest possibility of Susan being pregnant for they both knew he had not sought the warmth of her twin bed for at least three months before that fatal evening. It was perfectly possible that he would accuse her of promiscuity with another man.

Even if she told him exactly what had taken place during the period of time which was now a blank spot in his memory, she doubted whether he'd believe it to be true. Far more probable that he would accuse her of fabricating the whole story, to cover her own sins.

What *was* she to do?

She turned the problem over in her mind for a very long time and came to the conclusion that she should do nothing towards telling Glyn until she had ascertained for herself whether she was pregnant. She was almost positive but a visit to the doctor was clearly indicated.

I mustn't see our own G.P.! she decided suddenly, for he might inadvertently let slip the truth to Glyn, and that she did not want. If anyone was to tell him, then she was the person.

Later that evening she went to a pharmacist in the High Street to enquire the names of any doctors prepared to take private patients. The assistant was very helpful, consulting lists that were kept in the office, and then gave her the names and addresses of two doctors. She thanked the girl, and then went to the phone-box. Her appointment was for two o'clock the following afternoon.

The intervening twenty-four hours passed very slowly, but Susan used them to plan her campaign. She decided not to use her married name, as the Mohrs' was a familiar one in the city, with their great factory spreading across many acres on its outskirts. Her maiden name, perhaps? No. Better to use the word "Moore" ... same name, different spelling. Nothing to connect her with Edward or Glyn now.

She would tell the doctor that she had only just moved to the city and had not yet had time to find a house or a local G.P. That would prevent him from following up her case, and she would be the only one to know the truth until she had found some easier way of breaking the news to Glyn.

The doctor was kind and Susan wished she did not have to deceive him. He made a brisk examination and while she was getting dressed again, he said:

"Yes, Mrs. Moore, I think we can put the date of birth in January. Late January. I'll look in my book and give you a more approximate date in a minute. Of course," he added, smiling, "we can never say for sure which day baby will put in an appearance, because they like to arrive when they want to! Especially first babies. Would you like me to arrange for you to go into one of the private nursing homes for your confinement? Arrangements have to be made early, you understand, and I can give you the names of two who would take you as a paying patient. On the other hand, if you prefer to use the very excellent facilities offered by the Health Service, either in a hospital or having the baby in your own home, then I suggest that you find a panel doctor in the district you're hoping to live. He can make all the arrangements for you, and look after you during the very important prenatal period." He smiled again. "Having a baby as a paying patient can be an extremely expensive business, Mrs. Moore."

"I understand," Susan replied. "I'll discuss it with my husband and I expect we'll join a National Health doctor's panel."

"Splendid! Now, I'll write a letter for you to give

your new doctor. Just sit down, and I won't be long."

Five minutes later, Susan emerged into the bright sunshine, the promised letter clutched in one hand, and a receipt for the consultation in the other. She walked blindly towards the bus stop. It was true! There was no doubt about it. She was going to have Glyn's baby. The knowledge gave her a warm, comforting feeling. Whatever happened now, she would always have something of Glyn's. No one could ever rob her of this part of him

At home she ordered tea which Elsie, the maid, brought into the lounge. As she drank the refreshing liquid, she pondered her next move. It was essential that she spoke to Glyn. It was ridiculous to hope that he might open his arms and draw her to him ... the past forgotten.

It was possible that he didn't want either her or the child. In that case, she certainly had no intention of placing him under any kind of obligation to her. She still had her pride, if nothing else.

For over half an hour she sat looking at the telephone, wondering whether to ring him or go round to see him in person. The disadvantage of calling at his parents' home was the question of whether they would allow her to speak to him alone. On the phone she might have a little privacy. Whichever method she used, she had to speak to Glyn.

At last she took the plunge and lifted the receiver, dialling her in-laws' home number. The maid answered and she asked to speak to Mr. Glyn Mohr.

"One moment please, Madam. Who is calling?" Susan gave her name and the maid put down the receiver. With heart in mouth and almost sick with apprehension, Susan waited. She played a childish mental game: the longer I wait, the more likely it'll be Glyn who comes! She strained her ears for the sound of a limping man but soon, all too soon, she heard the swift treads of a heavy walker. The receiver was snatched up and Edward's gruff voice bellowed in her ear:

"Now look here, Susan, Glyn and I have asked you to leave us alone, and that includes telephone calls."

"I'd like to speak to him, please," she requested firmly.

"Well you can't. He doesn't want to speak to you. Tell me what you've got to say, and make it brief. I'm a busy man."

"Does Glyn know I'm on the phone?" Susan persisted.

"Naturally. The maid knows her duty. However, my son has refused to accept your call. What do you want?"

Susan knew when she was beaten.

"It's nothing, Mr. Mohr. Nothing important," she murmured quietly and replaced the receiver in its cradle. Then she sank onto the settee and cried as if her heart would break.

It was useless ... quite useless! Glyn didn't care what happened to her. Therefore it would be better for him to remain in complete ignorance about the baby. There was really no need for him ever to find out because she would go far, far away, and cut herself free from the chains that held her. She must make a new life for herself and the baby. She must eject Glyn from mind and memory, and live only for *her* baby! It would be hers and hers alone. She need never share it with anyone ... not even her own mother.

Half an hour later there was a ring at the front door bell. Susan heard Elsie cross the hall, and wondered who could be calling at this time of the late afternoon. She hoped it was nobody important because she did not feel up to seeing anyone. Then she heard Elsie's soft voice and deeper tones, arguing. The door was thrown open and Edward Mohr pushed past the protesting Elsie. He flung his hat down on a chair and kicked the door shut with his foot. He leaned over the back of the settee glaring down at Susan's startled face and began:

"I'll not beat about the bush with you, young woman. Neither will I tolerate you phoning my house and upsetting my son, who is still far from well, as you should know! I think he's told you in no uncertain terms that he'll have nothing further to do with you, which includes phone calls and personal visits. I wasn't prepared to discuss the matter over the telephone for my servants to overhear, that's why I'm here now." He put his hand inside his breast pocket and drew out a folded piece of paper which he opened in front of her. She saw it was a check.

"I presume you wanted to discuss money with Glyn, so I'm here in his stead. Look at it!" he ordered. "I've made it out for a sum to keep you in sufficient comfort for a few years." He waved it under her nose. "Go on, girl, look at it! Or isn't it enough for you?" he added cruelly. "Don't pretend this amount is unsatisfactory."

Susan recoiled, horrified.

"I ... I," she began, then closed her mouth

firmly. Under ordinary circumstances nothing on earth would have made her even consider accepting such an enormous amount of money from anyone, least of all Edward Mohr. Between yesterday and today, everything had undergone an abrupt change. The future had been clearly mapped out for her. She was expecting Glyn's child, and naturally she would need money for it. The two of them had to live and eat and she could not now return to work. She had a very small sum of money that Glyn had settled on her; in addition there was the large amount he had put into the bank a week before the accident. She could leave that where it was, with a Banker's Order to continue the regular payments to her mother which she had not stopped after her marriage.

Accepting money from Edward was a different matter. In an inexplicable way, she felt obliged to accept it, because he had been instrumental in wooing Glyn away from her. He owed her more than he could ever give.

Calmly she stretched out her hand and said:

"Very well, Mr. Mohr. I'll take this. But not for the reason you think. If it gives you any satisfaction to feel you've 'bought me off', as I believe the saying is, then I trust you'll enjoy the pleasure it gives you. However, it's possible the day may arrive when you realize exactly what you've done by offering me this money."

"I very much doubt it!" Edward sneered, and a grim smile spread across his heavy features. "Just as I'd always expected. It was our money you were really after, not our son. He's well rid of you." He picked up his hat and prepared to leave, adding:

"You realize, I hope, that now you have money, you can't continue to live on here?"

The futility of Edward's words struck Susan as being very amusing. She threw back her head and laughed.

"Believe me, Mr. Mohr, the sooner I can leave here the happier I'll be!"

Edward snorted angrily and showed himself out.

Well, she had done it now! What was the next move? There was little time to waste.

CHAPTER TEN

Susan's most immediate problem to be resolved was the question of finding somewhere to live. She wanted to leave the city. The possibility of meeting either Glyn or his friends was too great, and she needed to forget him completely. Some small country town perhaps? A place where she was unknown and had never visited.

The morning after Edward's visit Susan went out and bought copies of as many national newspapers as possible, and any women's magazines containing likely advertisements. She spent the remainder of the day poring over the closely printed pages. She had almost given up in despair when she came across something which seemed the very answer to her prayers:

"Wanted urgently. Suitable tenant. Three-year lease. Coastal village cottage. Two beds, living, kitchen, all mod. cons. Owner going abroad. Swift settlement imperative. — Box 5978."

Susan went to the writing-desk and wrote to the number given in the advertisement. She hoped there would not be too many applicants and wondered where the coastal village was situated.

Three days later, her query was answered. A letter came from a small Cornish village that Susan had never heard of previously. Hastily she took out the road maps Glyn kept in the desk, and found it tucked away between high cliffs about ten miles from the nearest market town. Then she read the letter. It was warm and friendly, asking her to call at the address given as soon as it was convenient.

As soon as it was convenient! That would be to-morrow. Excitement surged through Susan. She must book a seat on the Paddington-Penzance express which stopped at the station in this city, and make arrangements to spend at least one night away from home. She doubted if it would be possible to do the two journeys in one day as she did not wish to overtax herself during the early stages of her pregnancy.

The train was half-full, and she found her seat easily. On reaching her destination she found that there was a bus waiting to take her, and the people who had travelled into the market town to do their shopping, back to the village. A deeply sunburned old man helped her lift her light suitcase aboard, and then assisted her into a seat near the door. The bus was full and everybody seemed to know everyone else. During the journey, purchases and prices were discussed and compared. Also relatives' complaints, and the latest additions to families both in the village and the town, and who was planning to take in summer visitors and who was not.

Susan was deeply interested. They seemed a happy, carefree group of folk; a community, in fact. Many cast quick glances at her, nodding a salutation with a smile. Just before she reached the village, she asked the conductor if he could recommend a hotel where she might stay overnight.

"There's only the 'Pinhay Arms'," he said. "We'll be stopping right outside, Ma'am, so you shouldn't be 'aving any trouble finding it. Bob Slater's the landlord. Course, it isn't exactly an hotel, jes' the local inn, but they say the beds are wonderful."

Susan was enchanted with the inn. The ceilings were low and oak-beamed. Everywhere brass shone, and the doors had latches instead of handles. Bob Slater showed her to a small room overlooking the harbor, where blue cornflowers in a glass vase embellished the wide window-sill. The curtains were gaily colored and both windows were open wide to welcome the sunlight. The murmur of the sea and the lazy cry of the gulls drifted in from outside.

Downstairs, Susan asked to be directed to the cottage.

"Ah, you'm be coming to live there, may be?" Bob Slater nodded his head knowingly. "The Baileys be sailing next week and I know them to be keen to find someone quick-like. Haven't found anyone to their liking yet, so I'm told." He wiped the back of his hand across his mouth, and said: "Go outside the door, Mrs. Moore, then turn right. Walk about 'undred yards till you gets to the cottage with the blue door. Mrs. Gerraty's white cat'll be sitting outside. Always does, so there won't be any mistaking the place. Then walk on till you comes to the gate leading to the field where Farmer Buse keeps 'is cows, and Bailey's cottage be the second one to your left.''

Susan thanked him demurely, although she badly wanted to laugh. She doubted if she would ever find her way after such directions. To her amazement, everything was as Bob Slater had said, even to the somnolent white cat.

The Baileys' cottage was small and set a little way back from the road. A creaking gate which needed oiling opened onto a crazy-paving path edged with green glass globes. A wide arch of honeysuckle tumbled over the front door. Instead of a knocker, there was a large ship's bell. All the windows upstairs and down were wide open and, from inside Susan could hear the strains of music. The radio, probably.

Almost at once the front door was opened by a small, fat woman with a smiling, suntanned face who greeted her:

"I'm Mrs. Bailey. You must be Mrs. Moore. We received your postcard this morning. I'm so glad you could come. Did you have a good journey down? Not too crowded, I hope?'' Susan answered each of the questions and found herself being ushered through a small hall towards a large room overlooking the garden at the back of the cottage.

She gasped with pleasure. It was a beautiful room, with two sets of french windows opening onto the well-kept garden which sloped gently away from the house towards the cliffs so that a good expanse of the harbor and surrounding district could be seen. The room itself was comfortably furnished, with good quality mats on a dark polished floor. A small, equally plump man stood puffing his pipe by one of the windows. Susan was introduced to Mr. Bailey and talked to him while his wife hustled away to prepare tea for their visitor.

Sitting in a chintz-covered armchair sipping a cup of hot, sweet tea, Susan sighed with delight. Mrs. Bailey beamed and offered her a plate on which lay thick chunks of saffron cake. Susan took a slice but refused the clotted cream offered with it.

"Ah, you'll have to get used to lots of cream if you mean to live here!" Mrs. Bailey chuckled. "We all live on it. Does you the power of good, doesn't it, George?" Her husband smiled, lifting his eyes for a moment from the task of spreading an enormous layer of the cream on top of his wedge of cake.

"Shall miss it while we're away, make no mistake!" he grumbled. Susan liked cream but at the present time she preferred not to risk upsetting her already queasy stomach with too much richness. Later, perhaps, when the first four months had passed and she was feeling better.

The Baileys and Susan discussed the tenancy agreement and rent over the tea-table. Afterwards, Mrs. Bailey showed her over the rest of the cottage. The two bedrooms were small but ideal for Susan's purpose and the bathroom diminutive but adequate. The kitchen, however, was a dream, for, as her hostess explained, she believed in having as many of the latest gadgets as she could fit into the space provided by the recent modernization of the cottage. The stairs were narrow and steep but Susan knew she would be able to negotiate them with care.

When they were in the lounge again, Susan said:

"Before I accept your very generous offer, I feel I must be fair and ask one question. Have you any objections to a child living here? You see, although I'm separated from my husband, I'm expecting his baby."

"Oh you poor dear!" soothed Mrs. Bailey, putting a motherly arm around Susan's shoulders. "How could any man do such a cruel thing to his wife at such a time!"

"Miriam! I hardly think it's any affair of ours," her husband admonished.

"I'm sorry, my dear. It's just that George and I adore children and never had the good fortune to have any of our own. Now, of course, it's far, far too late to even think of adopting a baby."

Susan sympathized with her hostess and could not help noticing by the way they glanced at each other that the two grey-haired folk obviously adored one another. The lack of a family had not caused any rift, she thought enviously. If only she and Glyn had been as happy as the Baileys!

Their business quickly settled, the Baileys offered to put Susan up for the night, but she regretfully declined, explaining that she already had a room at the inn and hoped to catch the early bus to be at the station in plenty of time for the train the following morning. Her host and hostess insisted that she have supper with them, and this she gladly accepted.

When they parted later that evening, Susan felt strangely at peace. She had not known such happiness. Within two weeks she would be living here!

The following ten days flew by as Susan made her preparations. After a great deal of deliberation, Susan decided to keep the name of "Moore". Later on, when the baby had been born, she would have to give the name of its father to the registrar of births ... she could revert to the correct spelling just for that one occasion, perhaps. Anyhow, she'd think of it when the time came.

She gave Elsie and the cleaning woman four weeks pay in lieu of notice, and completely cleared the house of her own personal belongings. They fitted into a large trunk and two small suitcases. She sent the former in advance to Cornwall.

Then there was the question of her car. In the village she would have no use for it. The bus service into the town was regular and she hoped to travel there only once in a while when the need arose. Besides, with a pram, there would be no need to keep on the car, even if she could afford the motor-tax and insurance. The latter was unwarranted, and the money of far more use. She drove the car to a local garage and asked them to make her an offer for it.

What was she to do about her bank accounts? If she transferred them there was always the possibility of one or the other of the Mohrs tracing her through the bank, and this she would not tolerate.

In the manager's office, Susan spoke frankly. She told him she wished to transfer the entire value of Edward Mohr's cheque to the branch in the market town near where she intended to live. She wisely did not give him the name of the village, and informed him that on no account was he to divulge her whereabouts to any member of the Mohr family.

A taxi came to take her to the station. As she locked the front door for the last time, she felt no regrets whatsoever. It had been an unhappy house, and she was thankful to leave it. She put the key in an evelope and asked the taxi driver to take her by a roundabout route to the station so that she could leave the key at Glyn's solicitor's office. This accomplished, she sat back. The house and its contents were no longer her responsibility.

She reached the station in good time and soon was moving westwards, to a completely new life.

CHAPTER ELEVEN

For the first week, Susan explored the village and surrounding countryside. She familiarized herself with the whereabouts of the shops, and also went into town where she opened a bank account. The bank manager was pleased to accept her transfer and, on request, made several excellent suggestions on how she should best invest the money Glyn's father had given her. He did some quick figuring and Susan was surprised to find out exactly how much these investments would bring in. Naturally, it wouldn't be a fantastic sum, but sufficient for the time. Wisely, she also kept a small amount of capital available should she need some in a hurry. With care and economy, she decided she would be able to live without having to work before the baby's arrival. Afterwards ... that was a different problem, and one she would tackle the following year.

The village was beautiful. It hugged the steep sides of the valley, with the houses and cottages built

almost on top of one another from the water's edge.
The harbor was calm and serene, with boats of all
kinds bobbing quietly at anchor or tied up to the harbor walls. Some of the cottages clung like limpets to
the waterside, so that Susan could well imagine sitting in the window seat of one of their many bay windows and pretending she was on board an old tall
master. White-stuccoed, or grey block, timber-faced,
and all slate roofed, their windows were small-paned,
casement or sash-cord. There was a unity about the
village that impressed Susan. Everyone seemed to
know everyone else.

A family of graceful swans ruled the harbor waters
and the stream tumbling down the hillside towards
the sea. They gathered beneath the overhanging
windows in the evenings, waiting for someone to
throw out pieces of bread for them. They were sleek,
healthy birds.

There were also the small boys who, when they
were not attending school during the daytime, spent
hours in the water, shouting and splashing each
other. Susan smiled to see their immense enjoyment.
Gulls stood about on the houseroofs, chimneys, harbor walls and ships' masts; waiting. They were always
waiting. They seemed to sense the arrival of the
fishing boats from a long way off, because they would
fly around the harbor, screeching excitedly before
coming to roost on the housetops nearest the water.
When the catches were being brought ashore, there
were gulls everywhere, snatching bits and sometimes
whole fish, and quarrelling incessantly.

Susan was surprised to discover how much the
village folk seemed to know about her, although she

herself had told them nothing. They were gentle and kind to her, stopping to pass the time of day and to ask if she had settled down in her new home. She began to suspect that her absent landlord and his wife had supplied the villagers with details about their tenant. However, this did not worry her at all. In one way it was a blessing in disguise, for she was not subjected to questions on her past home and kind enquiries of the sort that might embarrass her.

She swiftly discovered a very pleasant walk. Instead of going down the hill into the village, she turned away from it and struck out for the open cliffs beyond. About a quarter of a mile away from her cottage she found a wide cliff path which led down to a beach. There was also another path which continued westwards, following the configuration of the coastline. The beach was only visible at low tide, she discovered, for when it had turned, the sea soon came right up to the harsh rocks at the foot of the cliff. She liked to sit on the green, springy turf at the cliff edge and watch the foam as it crawled sixty feet below. The spume was like long fingers, seeking and searching, feeling its ways against the rock barrier. She could well imagine how, on rougher days, it would crash up against those same rocks, tilting skywards to a great height before turning slowly and then descending in a tumult of boiling sand-flecked foam.

It was when she was up on the cliff alone, with only the whisper of the sea for company and the cry of a bird above, that Susan found herself thinking again and again of Glyn and the life she had left. Those few months together had been so full of artificiality, with strange, bored faces around her ... some of whose names she could barely remember after even this short time ... soon she would have forgotten them all. They had meant nothing to her, neither she to them. The news of her separation must have ceased to be a seven days wonder long ago. Even now she could imagine some of those overdressed, artificial women saying in lanquid voices:

"Susan Mohr? Who on earth is that?"

Yet the memory of Glyn was still very close. She could not prevent herself from wondering how he was. Was he missing her at all? No, that was quite impossible. She missed him terribly, especially now that the baby was growing so fast within her. At home, if she wanted to, she could always take the photo she had of him from the drawer and look at it. Yet she tried to resist such temptation. Better to leave it where it was, face down under a pile of clothes.

If only she had tried to understand him while they had lived together! She realized that they had both been equally to blame for their failure; at the same time, she knew that if she had really made the effort instead of resenting him so bitterly, she might have been able to find some way of beginning to put matters right. She had done nothing constructive whatsoever. She also wondered if she should write and tell her mother what had happened, but decided against it. The time was not yet ripe. She could not have found the words.

It was on one of her walks during the second week that she almost had a very nasty accident. She had reached the cliff top and was standing near the edge, looking out to sea at a lone yacht. The sea breeze gently ruffled her hair and blew her cotton dress against her legs. She lowered her gaze and riveted it on the beach below her. The sand was yellow and wet, unsullied by footprints. The tide was almost out but here and there it curled and sucked around the black rocks. Out of the blue, a fierce wave of faintness assailed her. The world began to sway and mist. She knew she had to come away from the edge before she toppled over, but somehow her feet were too weak to move. The stretch of sand seemed to be coming nearer, stretching up to touch her, to draw her down to itself. She put a hand to her head, panic-stricken.

I mustn't fall! I've got to move back!

Gasping for breath, she heard footsteps running behind her and a strong arm shot out to envelop her. She was jerked roughly to one side whereupon blackness overcame her. When she came to she found herself with her head being forced between her knees and a stern voice commanding her to take great gulps of air. The voice went on in a friendlier tone, although it was still scolding:

"That edge is very crumbly, you know. It's very unwise to stand as near as you were."

Susan struggled to sit up properly, her senses fully recovered. Then she turned to look at her rescuer. He was crouching at her side, watching her carefully. She was struck at once by the sincerity in a pair of wide-set green eyes, thick eyebrows and a humorous mouth. His face was almost girlish in shape but there was a determination about the forehead that assured her he was a man not to be trifled with. He looked about thirty, she decided dreamily. His face broke into a smile.

"Better now?" he asked, and his fingers closed

over her wrist, feeling for her pulse. She looked down at her hand and then back at him.

There was an unspoken question in her gaze.

"Are you . . .?" she began. He nodded.

"Yes. Doctor Roger Harlow. I know you, naturally. You're our new neighbor, Mrs. Moore. How do you do?" He slipped his hand down from her wrist to shake hers. Susan laughed.

"How do you do?" she replied. "This is a strange place to be introduced!" Roger Harlow changed his crouching position, sitting down to stretch his legs out in front of him. He heaved a sigh of relief.

"That's more like it!" Leaning back on the turf, he rested his chin on his hand and looked at Susan. His eyes were screwed up against the sun's glare. "In future, if you've this tendency to vertigo in high places, you must be careful not to wander too near cliff edges."

"Oh, I don't suffer from that complaint!" she protested, then blushed quickly. His eyes were twinkling and his voice teased. "Now don't tell me that our newest neighbor was actually thinking of *jumping* off that edge?" The ludicrousness of his suggestion made her throw back her head and roar with laughter, as he had intended it should.

"Of course not! Surely it didn't look as if I would? By the way, where *did* you spring from? I thought I was all alone here today."

"As a matter of fact, it's my free afternoon. For a change, instead of my usual sailing expedition, I decided to amble up here." He yawned. "Sorry, that was rude of me. I was up late last night coping with a particularly tough delivery, and I felt far too tired to get the dinghy out. Pure laziness, naturally. Still, perhaps it was a good thing I changed my mind. Otherwise there could have been a very unpleasant accident."

"I'm glad you came along, and thank you for what you did just now. I promise not to stand near cliff edges in future."

"Splendid."

"And you're the village doctor?"

"One of them, the junior partner. My boss is a good man, getting on for retirement shortly but still as fit as a fiddle and eager for hard work."

"I've been meaning to come to the surgery because I must register with a doctor fairly soon."

"And we'll be delighted to accept you, Mrs. Moore. I'll care for you myself, if you wish, or my partner will have you as his patient."

"Thank you, but I think I'd like your services, if I may?"

Roger Harlow grinned.

"Before we start, I should warn you that I've the advantage over you, Mrs. Moore. The Baileys and I are very great friends, and it seemed only natural for them to tell me all about their successor. I'm delighted to add that they didn't exaggerate those glowing reports."

Susan blushed.

"Mrs. Bailey was quite right. She said you were very charming and beautiful."

Susan wondered if he realized he had given her an opening.

"Did . . . did she also tell you about my husband?" After all, as her medical adviser, he would have to be told sooner or later.

"Yes. She said you were separated and expecting your first baby. She also told me ... and this is strictly off the record ... that I was to take the greatest possible care of you otherwise I'd have her wrath to contend with when she eventually returns to England!"

Susan laughed.

"How kind of her. I'm glad she told you everything because it makes it all so much easier for me." His eyes twinkled mischievously.

"I expect that if we hadn't met today I should have made it my duty to call on you in any case. My partner and I are most particular about our expectant Mums. We don't like them to be left without prenatal care for any length of time in case anything should be neglected."

Susan's mouth twitched, and she scolded:

"I understand, Doctor. You were going to pay me a visit in order to persuade me to join your panel. In other words, you were cadging for trade. Scandalous, Doctor, absolutely scandalous! I've a good mind to report you to the Medical Council, or whatever is the disciplinary board."

Roger pretended to look hurt.

"Madam, you've misunderstood me completely. I'd never even consider the remotest opportunity of canvassing for 'trade' as you so delicately put it. No, I was acting as a good neighbor to a stranger in our midst." His voice became serious. "Mrs. Moore, you must book early for a hospital bed, you know. Anyway, I'm off duty now, perhaps you'll call at the surgery soon? You'll find it in the double cottage at the bottom of Macken's lane, that's the turning three doors down from the smithy, so you won't miss it."

"Also, my dear Mrs. Moore, neither I nor my partner can risk losing a patient up here. It would look so terribly bad for business!"

"I'm not on your panel ... yet," she reminded him gently.

"Just think how appalled the villagers would be to learn of the sudden and unexpected demise of our newest arrival ... and the most attractive one, too!"

She laughed.

"You flatter me."

"Only on my free afternoons. When I'm on duty, then my behavior is strictly professional. Of course, the great advantage of a country practice like mine lies in the fact that we can get to know our patients, and they us. Here they're not merely names in a massive filing cabinet as I fear is bound to happen in the large cities. Our patients are people who are born, live, breathe, worry, rejoice, make love, age, and eventually die. Each of my patients is unique and I try to learn as much about them as I can so that when they need me, I can be a real help, not just for their physical ills, but also their mental, and occasionally spiritual welfare. There, I've said enough. Now you're looking very much better. May I walk home with you, if you're thinking of returning?"

"Please do," Susan replied, adding shyly: "Perhaps you'd care for a cup of tea?"

"An excellent suggestion."

They walked slowly back to Susan's cottage, during which time she learned that Roger had qualified four years previously but had not yet yearned to specialize as had so many of his colleagues.

"No. All I cared for was to leave the filth and

bustle of the cities and find myself some nice, quiet country practice. It was more by luck than by good management that I came here. Dr. Thomas, he's my partner, needed a younger man because his former partner was retiring early through ill-health. This man was a distant relative of one of the chaps I studied with, and he was asked if he'd care to take over. He loathed the idea, having set his heart on chest surgery, but fortunately he remembered my own yen for the wild, open spaces. I applied, with a helpful letter of introduction from my colleague as well, and Dr. Thomas accepted me at once."

"You like the life here?"

"Love it. My parents were very good. They lent me money with which to purchase the cottage, and I often go up to the old house on the hill to see the man whose place I took. He's bedridden now, of course, but is still very agile mentally. My cottage is built beside the stream, tucked right in behind a row of shops. I expect you've seen it; cream colored walls and a scarlet front door, with wisteria running riot all over the place and keeping my rooms well supplied with spiders and insects!"

"Do you look after yourself or are you married?"

"No and no. I've a woman who comes in every day. I have two sisters, both of whom I adore, but they don't visit me very often. At the beginning they did. In fact, I could hardly ever get rid of the blighters!" He laughed. "As soon as they learned that I was living by the sea, then they both developed a passion for sailing and fishing. They came to stay for months on end during the summer. That stopped two years ago, and I'm now left in peace."

"Didn't it work out?" Susan enquired gently.

"Oh yes, we all got on like a house on fire, until they suddenly found other interests in the male forms of Hugh and Jack. They're married now. Marian has had two children in quick succession, while Elaine has one daughter and is expecting another child in the late spring. Thanks to Hugh and Jack, I'm now well free of my adorable sisters, although I suspect that when their children are not very much older, I shall be inundated with requests to allow them to stay here for their holidays. It wouldn't surprise me, of course, to learn that my two scheming sisters have already drawn up the rota of who shall descend on me first and who second!" He opened the creaking gate. "Well, that just about finishes my saga."

They went inside the cottage and Susan put the kettle on.

"How do you like living in this cottage?" Roger asked.

"I love it. It's such a happy little house!"

"You're very lucky to get it. I've always looked upon it as being one of the village's nicest. It has such an excellent view and you haven't far to go to the shops and the quay. Also, and it's a great blessing, you're spared the visitors' cars parked right outside. Very few come this way out of the village, the road is too narrow and winding, leading nowhere."

"Since I've been here, I haven't seen very many holidaymakers."

"The bulk of them'll be arriving soon. The worst weeks are the last two in July, right through to the end of August. Then we get hordes of trippers."

Susan's face fell.

"Milk and sugar?" she asked.

"Please."

"I was told we were too far off the beaten track to be inundated with holidaymakers."

He grinned.

"Yes, I suppose we are. I'm sorry. I was pulling your leg. The lack of holiday facilities here saves us from too many visitors, although sufficient arrive to satisfy the villagers who cater for them. People like Amanda Porter and her mother who run the tea-shop on the quay. There are always folk who come in cars from the towns and inland places. Some of them seem to find a tremendous fascination in watching the fishermen unload their catches, and they'll stand on the quay for hours on end, just looking. The people who want sea and sand for their youngsters usually stop at the beach four miles away. So we're spared most of them, because the thought of walking four miles in search of a cup of tea on a boiling hot afternoon doesn't appeal to many folk!"

"Why don't they use the lovely stretch of sand here?" Susan asked.

"It's only visible at low tide, and no one can swim from the rocks when the tide's in because the undertow's far too treacherous."

He declined a further cup of tea.

"I must leave now," he said, standing up reluctantly. "Thanks very much for the happy hour I've spent in your company, Mrs. Moore. Now, don't forget to come to the surgery to see one of us. Nine till ten, or six to seven in the evenings."

Susan saw him to the door and stood to watch him

as he strode down the lane into the village, covering the distance in quick, long strides. Then she went inside again.

Suddenly she realized that during the time they had been together this afternoon, she had not once thought of Glyn.

CHAPTER TWELVE

Two mornings later, Susan visited Roger Harlow professionally. He filled in a card, asking relevant questions; childish ailments, other serious illnesses, vaccinations, etc., name and address of nearest relative, but this she declined to give. He made no comment, merely pausing to peer at her for a moment over the top of the thick-rimmed spectacles he now wore Then he asked her to prepare herself for examination while he read the letter she had brought him from the private doctor who had confirmed her pregnancy When it was over, he said:

"Everything's progressing very satisfactorily, Mrs. Moore. Now we must decide what arrangements to make for the actual birth. Where would you like to have the baby? Before you say anything, I must tell you that we've an excellent midwife here, and I also know someone who'd be only too willing to act as home-help during the few weeks after the birth." He smiled gently. "Amanda's an absolute gem! I think I mentioned her the other day. She and her mother run the tea-shop. It's closed from mid-September till Easter every year, and therefore Amanda's free.''

Susan frowned.

''I assure you, Mrs. Moore, you'll lack for nothing with Amanda to care for you. I've often used her services during the winter months for my home confinements. A great many of our patients insist on staying home so that she can be called in. I suspect many of them of arranging their babies to fit in with Amanda's free months. She's a hard worker and a marvel with children. Also, her charges are reasonable.

''If you'd rather have the baby in hospital, I should warn you that it's over ten miles away, which is really too far in the case of emergency. Some of my Mums haven't even had the consideration to wait until they've passed through the hospital gates, and an ambulance has been known to pull into the side of the main road to attend to an impatient baby! I'd like you to think about it for a day or two, and then let me know, unless of course you've made up your mind already that you prefer hospital? Or, if you'd like to, do call on Amanda to discuss my suggestion.''

Susan did not need extra time to make up her mind.

''I'd like to see your friend.''

''Good. I'll pop in and tell her to expect you, may I?''

''Please!''

Susan called at the tea-shop just before eleven the following morning. It was an attractive little place, right on the harbor. The windows were large, to let in plenty of light, and the tables of dark mahogany shone with polish, and on each stood a small bowl of wild flowers. The dark-green door stood open, although a notice plainly indicated that tea was not served until three in the afternoon. A yellow board sign, in the shape of a beehive, proclaimed its name.

The "Honeypot"

Susan stepped over the slate doorstep and knocked on the door. A small boy carrying an enormous basket over one arm, came towards her and bid her a cheery "good morning" before he rushed out into the open, whistling piercingly. He was followed by a tall, red-haired girl whose face broke into a welcoming smile.

"Mrs. Moore! Roger's told me to expect you. Do come in. Mind the boxes," she pointed to a pile of empty cartons lying just inside the tea-room. Then she led the way through a swing door into the kitchen at the back of the building. Mrs. Porter was working at the table, a rolling-pin in her hand. Her face was warm and flushed from the heat of the ovens. Wire trays of biscuits, buns and scones stood in rows to cool.

"Mum, this is Mrs. Moore," Amanda introduced them, and pulled out a chair for Susan.

"I see you're very busy. I shouldn't have come at such an awkward hour," she apologized but her hostess insisted she stay and have a cup of coffee with them. Amanda bustled around.

"We're well up to time today, and we don't open until three. Do you take sugar?"

Mrs. Porter then asked:

"You've come to discuss the new baby, bless its heart. Amanda'll be free in late January, so everything will be all right. Roger told us all about it yesterday and we'll do all we can to help you, dear."

Susan was overwhelmed with their kindness. She had taken an instant liking to Amanda. The younger girl sat on the edge of the table close to her and started to talk animatedly.

"I'll come any time you want me. Roger'll tell me nearer the actual date when I ought to be up at your cottage, so we can arrange all those details later on. You don't know anyone here, do you? We'll soon put that right. Roger's suggested I take you under my wing ... that's if you've no objection! ... and I'll be glad to do so. I suppose you started knitting ages ago?"

Susan had to admit that she had not even found any patterns.

"Never mind. Mrs. Arlen has plenty. She's in the haberdashery shop. I'll ask her to pop up to the cottage one evening with the book, shall I, then you'll be able to choose at leisure."

"Oh, I couldn't possibly impose on her!" Susan protested. "I'll go to her shop. Besides, it gives me an excuse to take some exercise."

They all laughed.

Susan's quiet manner and charm endeared her to all the villagers. It was not long before she knew most of them by their first names. Jamie Black, the milkman, a young, studious fellow who sported the most hideous ties Susan had ever seen ... when he wore one at all ... and who always picked out the largest eggs for her, and the thickest cream, while

Tom Jenkins the butcher cut off the most tender pieces of meat.

"Eating for two now," he'd say. "Only in quality but not in quantity, as Dr. Thomas always tells my missus when she's expecting."

Sometimes Reggie Scobbold, the fifteen-year-old son of one of the fishermen, would arrive on the doorstep and thrust a couple of fine fish into her hands before fleeing, crimson-cheeked. Neither was there ever a dearth of flowers in her vases. Her lawn was cut and the flower beds weeded by members of the local Scouts and Cubs. Often Jean Turner, the schoolgirl daughter of the baker, would bring in wild flowers that she had picked from the hedgerows on her way home from school.

She felt happy and contented, at peace with herself and the world. Her past unhappiness had faded to the back of her mind, and the trouble with Glyn was being dimmed by the passage of time.

After a great deal of heart-searching, she had eventually decided to write to her mother. In a long letter she told her exactly what had happened and that she had left Glyn. She did not mention the baby at all. She begged her mother to try to see things from her point of view and to understand her motives. She told her how sorry she was but it had seemed the only solution. This letter she enclosed in one to her bank manager in the city, giving no home address, and requesting him to send it on to her mother with the next payment from the account she had left untouched, the one Glyn had opened for her when they first married.

She began to attend church again, and it soon

became a regular Sunday habit. It gave her a great feeling of comfort, but also filled her with a sense of guilt for having neglected Sunday worship for so many years. It was Amanda who had persuaded her to go to church again.

When Roger was free, he would also join them as they trudged up the steep hill towards the church perched high above the village and harbor. Susan soon became conscious of the fact that Amanda was in love with Roger and was rather surprised he did not notice. It was in the way she looked at and spoke to him. His eyes, when they looked down at Amanda's eager face, were warm and amused, but Susan could detect no inner sign of love in them.

As for her own feelings towards him, she was not at all uncertain. She liked him tremendously. He was a good doctor and a kind friend. They had quickly forsaken the use of surnames, becoming Roger and Susan to each other. He was always considerate and gentle when they were together, yet at times, Susan was startled to see a quickly veiled expression of something just a little more than pure friendship in his eyes. Could it be that he was in love with her? She sincerely hoped not, for their relationship could never, never pass the bounds of deep friendship. She felt a moment of panic. She did not want Roger to love her! She belonged only to Glyn, regardless of whether he wanted her or not.

If only Roger could be made to love Amanda!

The heat of the summer passed, the last visitor left the village, the ''Honeypot'' put up its blinds, and cold winds and rain swirled in from the sea, greying everything. People scurried about with their collars turned up and heads covered, while the boats still moored in the harbor no longer rested quietly. Soon the fishermen dragged them onto higher ground, there to stay until the winter tides and storms had passed. The fishing vessels swung out of the agitated harbor waters into the roughness beyond, rearing and plunging as they strove seawards to cast their nets. Smoke belched from the cottage chimneys, to be whipped away by the fretful winds. Inside Susan's home all was snug and warm.

Now that her movements had become slower, Susan settled down to preparing for the baby. She bought wool and material, and spent long happy hours making baby clothes. She wondered what she should do about a cot and pram. Although she had a little extra money to draw upon, she did not want to use too much of it. The prices in the catalogs she had procured from the town seemed very high. It was too much to spend on one child. If she could only find someone with second-hand baby furniture to sell, her needs would be answered!

One afternoon, while Amanda was having tea with Susan, her problem was solved almost accidentally. She had left the catalogs on the table and had to move them before she could put down the tray. They were amongst a pile of magazines one of the villagers had lent her, and somehow they slipped from her arms and cascaded all over the floor. Amanda leapt to her rescue, picking them up for her as Susan was beginning to find it an effort to bend down these days.

Amanda found one of the catalogs and looked at it thoughtfully.

"This reminds me," she said. "You haven't

ordered one of these yet, have you?"

"No. Why?"

"Well, don't. I think I know of someone who has some second-hand stuff she'd like to be rid of, and quite cheaply too. Mind you," she added somewhat apologetically. "It's been used for two children, but there's still some life in it. Unless, of course, you're wanting to buy new?" She looked up at Susan whose face shone with relief.

"Oh no, I don't! That is, if I *can* buy second-hand, I'd far rather."

"Good. I know these people very well. Unfortunately, you know what most newly-married mums are like ... nothing but brand new so the bottom's virtually fallen out of the second-hand market. You ought to be able to purchase all of their baby stuff for give-away prices."

"Do you really think so?" Susan asked doubtfully

"Of course. I'll go and see them. What exactly will you be needing, do you think?"

"Pram. Cot. Ooh, and I'd better have a playpen and high chair because I can't allow the baby to mess up the Bailey's good furniture, can I?"

It was arranged that Amanda should let her know what she had been able to find out within the next week. What Susan did not learn, however, was that Roger had been inveigled into driving Amanda to the farmhouse to inspect some very battered and badly painted baby furniture.

"What do you think, Roger?"

"She'll never accept it in this condition! But if we take it back to my place, I think we could patch it up between the two of us."

Like conspirators in the night, they squeezed a cot, pram, playpen and high chair into Roger's station wagon, and whisked back to the village.

"None of it's very clean," Amanda said. "You give me a few days on this with soap and water and some paint, and we'll have it looking like new."

Three days later, Amanda brought Susan to Roger's cottage and showed her a wooden cot painted pale blue, a polished black pram with new wheels, and a varnished high chair and playpen. Susan was delighted.

"This is lovely!" she exclaimed. "How much did they want for it?"

"Five pounds the lot," the other girl lied glibly.

"Only five!"

"Yes. I paid for it then and there. You can refund whenever it suits you."

Susan was thrilled with her good fortune. Later, when they were alone, Roger said to Amanda:

"Now then, young lady, how much am I in your debt? We agreed to go fifty-fifty, remember?"

"Let me see, you gave the Walkers the five pounds they asked for, then there was the paint, varnish, new wheels and suspension straps, plus lots of new screws etc., etc. Here," she handed him a piece of paper with some figures scribbled on it. "This is only a very rough calculation."

He leaned over and tweaked her ear affectionately, then took out his wallet.

"Now remember, Amanda," he said as he handed her some money. "This is a secret just between you and me. Sue's pride would be terribly hurt if she ever found out what we'd been up to!"

Amanda stared up at him, searching his face thoughtfuly.

"You like her very much, don't you?"

He smiled.

"Yes."

She turned away, biting her lip.

"I see." Roger put his hands on her arms and turned her back to face him.

"Look at me, Amanda. There's one thing you and I must get straight. Sue's my *patient*, and you know darned well that we quacks aren't allowed to mix business with pleasure, therefore I have to be extremely careful in my dealings with her. No matter what private dreams and longings I might have, they must remain forever unfulfilled, for she already has a husband."

"I'm so fond of you!" Amanda murmured, burying her face in his jacket while he held her close, looking sadly into his eyes. "Please, please, don't get hurt!"

He touched her nose gently with one finger.

"You're very sweet, my dear, but you needn't worry about me. I can look after myself. As long as you're around to keep an eye on me!" he added, teasingly.

She would not smile.

"Don't go too far away, Roger!" she begged.

"I won't, I promise."

Amanda wisely let the matter rest there. With an experience beyond her years, she knew that whatever lay in Roger's system, only time would rid him of it and bring him back to her. Any foolish move now on her part might rob her of him forever. She must wait

As the weeks passed, Susan found she never had to

carry home any of her shopping because wherever she went there was always someone, young or old, ready to take her purchases. Many of the shopkeepers insisted on sending their goods up to the cottage by one of their numerous offspring. Since her arrival in the village she had become very popular and knew that behind her back the villagers referred to her as "Little Mrs. Widow". This touched her deeply, because she realized most of them had guessed the truth about her marriage.

Christmas approached, but she was not destined to spend it on her own. Mrs. Porter invited her to celebrate the festival with herself and Amanda. Roger came too, when he had finished his rounds. They all went to church in the morning and then sat down to turkey and Christmas pudding topped with brandy butter and thick cream. Roger drove her home early that evening, as she felt very tired these days. He came into the cottage with her, banked up the fire and refilled the coal scuttle, then made her a cup of tea.

When he had gone, she went upstairs. In her room, she opened the bottom drawer and took out Glyn's photo, carrying it to the bed-table so that she could inspect it more closely in the light of the lamp. Mentally she compared the two men in her life.

Roger, so kind, gentle and thoughtful, sincere in everything he said and did. Glyn, selfish to the core and often bitterly unkind. Pampered by his parents, and completely misunderstood by her.

She put down the photo and went over to the mirror to look at herself. Greedy for comfort, selfish and out for herself only. Resentful and not giving way one inch if she could possibly help it. But now, alas, fully aware of all her faults and a sadder but much wiser woman.

Yes, she and Glyn suited each other. Both full of unpleasant traits. If only he too had recognized himself for what he was, they might have had a chance together.

She loved him.

She bent her head and wept quietly.

CHAPTER THIRTEEN

The weeks following Christmas seemed to drag by unendingly. The weather became suddenly very cold, and it was an effort to negotiate the now slippery lanes. Susan longed to lose the burden within her, and wondered if every expectant mother felt as she was feeling towards the end of the nine months. She was often breathless and her head seemed to ache interminably.

One morning, while she was in the greengrocers, she collapsed and had to be taken home in the delivery van. Roger called almost immediately and ordered her to stay in bed until the baby was born.

"But it's not due for at least another fortnight!" she protested. "And we both know that first babies are notorious for their tardiness."

"Nevertheless, you'll stay where you are, Susan. Of course, if you take it into your head to disobey my orders, then I'll send you to hospital at once." He then dropped his stern tone. "Don't worry. I'll pop in and see Amanda. I'm sure she'll be able to come up here straightaway. She can use your other bedroom. The district nurse will be calling regularly, and I'll drop by whenever I'm passing. So you'll be in excellent hands, with absolutely nothing to do all day but read or knit. I wish it were me! I could do with a few days of laziness. I'll make out a prescription and Amanda'll bring it with her.''

For almost three weeks Susan found herself being treated like a queen. At first she thought she would hate having to keep to her bed, but after two days she began to enjoy herself and to feel thankful there were others to cope with her household chores. She felt much better, but only wanted to go on and on resting. Her blood pressure steadied and the ache left her head.

She told Amanda where to find the baby things, and together they discussed the last-minute arrangements and prepared everything that had to be done prior to the actual birth. It was while Amanda was hunting through the bottom drawer for some flannelette sheets to be put in the airing cupboard, that she accidentally drew out Glyn's photograph. Without really knowing what she was doing, she turned it over and looked at it.

Surprised at the sudden silence, Susan glanced up from the newspaper. Amanda swivelled round to face her, scarlet-cheeked and with the photo in her hands.

"I'm awfully sorry, Sue! I shouldn't have pried."

"May I have it, please?" Susan asked, her voice trembling. Amanda carried it to her.

"He's very good-looking!" she commented.

"Yes. I suppose he is." Susan took it, studying it

closely, seeing Glyn's face through the eyes of another. Whereas until just now she had noticed smoldering and scornful eyes, a firm chin and the overall domineering, arrogant expression, today she could see only a pleasant, good-featured handsome man. She placed the photo down on the bedspread and stared out at the snow-flecked sky beyond the window. A long, deep sigh escaped her lips. "Put it away again, there's a dear. Underneath all those clothes, at the back of the drawer."

She remained staring blankly into space while Amanda continued her business at the chest of drawers. Had it only been Christmas when she had last looked at Glyn's photo? When had she *really* thought about him since then? Her mind had been too full of thoughts of the coming baby, yet why was it that today old memories had been vividly revived? They were both bitter and sweet. This unintentional act on Amanda's part had brought Susan face to face once again with the harsh reality that she was missing Glyn intensely. At Christmas, she had known she was going to look at the photo; today it had been thrust upon her when she was totally unprepared.

Where was he now? How had the court case gone? She presumed the authorities must have been satisfied with the eyewitness's account of the accident, as her absence seemed to have been accepted without question. Was he still living with Edward and Beatrice? Did he ever think of her?

Amanda spoke to her, but she did not hear. The younger girl then regarded her thoughtfully for a moment, frowned, and went back to her work. Better to say nothing. It was perfectly plain that Susan had no desire to tell her anything else about her husband.

It was on a cold, sleety day that Susan's labor began. Amanda sent for the midwife and then went upstairs to help Susan. Roger looked in later in the morning, pronounced himself satisfied and then went home to lunch. Dusk came early, and an hour later Amanda came running from the cottage to fetch Roger.

Upstairs, Susan was past caring what happened to her. She was fed up with the whole, horrid business. Why was the baby so long in arriving? All around her was discomfort and utter weariness. She was so very tired!

The midwife bent over her, scolding.

"Mrs. Moore, you're fighting against the pains instead of using them."

"I don't care!" she wailed, full well realizing how foolishly she was behaving. She wept with frustration. Roger arrived and joined the midwife but his patient was too full of self-pity to notice anyone but herself and the anguish that was gnawing at her. Suddenly she called out:

"Glyn! I want Glyn! Where is he? Why isn't he here?"

Roger looked across to Amanda who had just come into the room carrying the bowl of instruments he had asked her to sterilize in case they should be needed.

"Glyn, is that you?" Susan called to her and stretched out her arms. "Help me! Hold my hand!"

"Should we send for her husband?" Amanda whispered to Roger.

"How can we? We've no idea where he lives or how to contact him."

"Please!" Amanda pleaded. "It might help her."

Roger grinned.

"By the time he gets here, it'll all have been over hours beforehand, by which time she'll have forgotten she even asked for him."

"We could still try!" she insisted. "Besides, it's *his* child and he ought to know about it."

"I wouldn't meddle, if I were you, love. However, if it's what you want, here goes." He bent over the patient. "Sue, tell me, where's Glyn? We'll send for him if you'd like us to."

Susan gripped his hand fiercely.

"No! No, he mustn't come here! He mustn't find me! He doesn't want me, and I haven't told him about the baby. Please, please don't send for him!" she begged, crying. Another spasm seized her.

"Mums!" Roger sighed, and then set to work as the birth appeared to be imminent.

Three-quarters of an hour later, Susan was delivered of a seven-and-a-half pound boy. She suddenly awoke, coherent again, and her face shone with wonderous delight as the midwife put her son into her arms.

"It's a fine boy!" she told her proudly.

"A son! I have a son!" Susan whispered and pressed her cheek against the new arrival's very soft skin. Then she slept the sleep of exhaustion.

When both mother and son had been made comfortable for the rest of the night, and the midwife had taken herself off home, Amanda sat with Roger in the quiet warmth of the kitchen where they both refreshed themselves with quantities of tea.

They did not talk much, for both were aware of the

deep companionship that enveloped them. Eventually, Amanda said:

"Susan's always wanted a boy, Roger. Her dream's come true. She has a son ... Glyn's son." She was watching Roger's face closely and could not mistake the sudden tightening of his lips. If she had had any doubts before, they were immediately set aside. Roger loved Susan. Her heart felt heavy enough to break, but she said nothing.

"Yes. We've had a successful night," was his comment after a long pause. "I've been thinking over Susan's plea first to send for her husband and then not to. It might have been better had she told us how to contact him. But she's never let drop even a hint about the place she used to live! Still, he has a right to know about his son," he finished thoughtfully.

"He's awfully good-looking, you know."

"Oh? And how do you know?"

Amanda told him about the photo she had found, adding:

"I think the hurt's still very near the surface, although she refuses to talk about him."

"Perhaps it would do her more good to tell someone," Roger suggested. "The hurt must be got out of her system; she can't go through life licking her wounds. Now she has the baby to live for. He'll help, naturally. Life has to go on regardless. Let's hope she'll soon realize it!"

Susan's baby was a very good child and presented her with no problems. He fed and slept well, continuing to grow and flourish. When he was six weeks old, Anthony John was christened in the church on the hilltop, with Roger and Amanda acting as godparents

for him. Amanda had offered to travel into town with
Susan on the day she wished to register the birth, but
the latter declined, asking her to babysit for her instead. At the registry, Susan gave the clerk the correct spelling of Glyn's surname. In the years to come,
of course, Tony might ask why the spelling had been
altered, but that wouldn't be for a very long time ...
not until he would need to present his birth certificate
to a future employer ... years and years hence. She
could forget about names for the present.

When the baby went out in his pram, the villagers
would stop to coo at him. He adored all the attention,
squirming about in the pram and showing toothless
gums in a wide, happy smile. Later, Susan discovered
he had a very infectious chuckle. She adored her
Tony.

Roger also thought the world of him, and made no
attempt to hide his affection. Amanda could not help
wondering whether he loved the baby for its own sake
or because he happened to be Susan's son. She knew
she was being unjust and jealous, and she hated
herself.

Roger made a point of popping into the cottage
regularly each day to see how his "Munchkin" was,
as he called Tony. Often, when he had a free afternoon, he would collect Amanda and together they
took Susan and the Munchkin for a walk.

Surprisingly, Amanda made no comments about
these walks, although her mother shook her head now
and again as she watched the quartet walk past the tea-
shop. Little did she realize that beneath her daughter's
happy smiling face there lay a heart of lead.

One April afternoon, when Tony was three months

old, and Amanda had to stay at home because her mother was not too well, Roger and Susan set out alone. The wind was brisk, but the sun was shining. Roger insisted on pushing the pram on his own towards the cliffs where they had first met. The view was magnificent, and it had become Susan's favorite spot, although she never went near the cliff edge. Later, when Tony was big enough for a stroller, she hoped to take him down onto the beach and let him play about on the sands.

Roger spread an old mackintosh on the ground, and they sat down to talk while Tony lay sleeping in the pram. He asked Susan what plans she had for the future. She smiled.

"Why should you think I've changed the ones I made almost a year ago? I'll continue to live here, naturally. Perhaps, when Tony's old enough to go to primary school I'll have to think about finding some kind of job. I don't know what I could do, because I only served in a shop before I became a second-rate model." She shrugged. "A very empty life, of course, but I can't do anything else. I wish now I'd had the sense and money to train as a secretary, but training takes time when the money's badly needed at home. Still, I suppose if I'd been really keen, I'd have attended night school after shop hours. However, I didn't, and that's that. Maybe I could teach myself typing and shorthand, although I doubt it. Also, I'd need a typewriter, and I don't want to spend money rashly. Tony needs my time and money at the moment."

"Can you do dressmaking?" Roger enquired.

"Not on your life!" Susan laughed. "I'm pretty hopeless with a needle. I can make little things, but nothing that has that important professional look you need if you're thinking of taking in work for other people. I couldn't possibly consider dressmaking as a means of making a living."

"Sue, forgive me for asking, but have you heard from your husband at all?"

She shook her head.

"No, Roger, and I don't want to. He doesn't know where I am, and I'm content to leave it that way."

"The night that young man arrived," Roger pointed to the pram, "you called out for Glyn. Do you remember?"

Susan's mouth opened in surprise.

"Did I really? My goodness! I've forgotten such a lot about the night Tony came."

"As I expected you to. At that stage of labor my Mums rarely remember anything at all of what they say or do." He laughed loudly. "Good thing they do, too! I feel sure if I listened to or repeated some of the language they used, I wouldn't have any patients left!" He picked up one of her hands and held it tightly. "I know I shouldn't be speaking like this, but I'm not on duty. Glyn, that's his name, isn't it? Don't you think it's time you made up your mind what to do about him?"

"How do you mean?"

"I know you're not completely happy. Have you considered your joint futures?"

"Surely there's nothing *to* consider? I've done everything I can."

"I know. But is a separation enough in itself? I mean, wouldn't you both be happier if you got a divorce, thus making the break clean?"

"Divorce can never be a 'clean' break, Roger," Susan said quietly, "as you should very well know. All kinds of unpleasantnesses are brought out into the open for everyone to talk about."

Roger was persistent.

"Yes, I know. Surely divorce would be better than this ... this emptiness of living apart?"

"I don't know, Roger. I honestly don't!"

"Besides, you're entitled to maintenance money, especially now you have Tony ""

Susan jerked her hand away.

"Glyn must never be told about him. He or his parents might try to take him away from me if they knew!"

"They couldn't do that, my dear," he soothed.

"Yes they could!" Susan was quite agitated. "You don't know their type. Glyn's always wanted a son and if he knew about Tony " she left the sentence unfinished.

"You needn't worry about me!" she continued bitterly. "I wouldn't come into their plans at all. You see, Glyn's father 'bought me off' with a very handsome sum. And I accepted it, but only because I knew Tony was on the way. Otherwise I wouldn't have touched a penny of his filthy money." Her voice had risen almost to a shriek. Roger took her hands firmly in his and held them tightly.

"Calm yourself, Sue, there's a good girl, or you'll wake the Munchkin and he'll cry. I realize you've had more than your fair share of trouble, but you must look at the problem from another angle. You're young, you have a bonny child, and you've got to think about him and his future. He needs a fatherly hand to guide him, as well as a mother's love. Don't you see how much better it would be for him to end your unhappy marriage?"

"Glyn can divorce me for desertion after three years are up." Her gaiety was false and bitter, and Roger knew she was close to tears.

"Now, if you were free ..." he murmured, staring out to sea, "but a man in my position doesn't talk of such things ..." He cleared his throat and went on in a different tone: "You know, Susan, happiness can be within your grasp, even though you may think it's nowhere near you. Look out there, where the sky meets the sea, in a firm, solid line. That's what happiness is ... a solid ring surrounding each and every one of us, if we're prepared to notice it."

"Is it?" Susan commented wryly. "How can it be tangible and within our grasp? The sky never actually meets the sea, as we all very well know. No matter where or how far we go in search of it, it's only an illusion. So's happiness ... a bitter illusion."

"No, darling Sue, it needn't be!" Roger said quickly. "Happiness is where you *want* it to be. If you make up your mind to get fulfilment from life, then happiness comes naturally. On the other hand, if you set out in deliberate pursuit of happiness, then it'll be as you say, just an illusion and forever beyond your grasp." He wrinkled his eyes and stared at her thoughtful face. "Is your future to be over there, where the sky meets the sea, or are you going to pass through life continually searching? Tell me, Sue, I need your answer!"

Bewildered and a little scared at the sudden passion in Roger's voice, Susan murmured:

"You're very sweet, but I'm not the woman for you! Amanda loves you, or didn't you know?"

"Amanda!" His face was stricken and he bit his lip. "What a fool I am not to realize. I should have known she wouldn't joke. The poor, dear child."

"Oh, you exasperate me beyond measure sometimes, Roger! Can't you get it into your head that Amanda isn't a child any longer? She's just as much a woman as I am. Don't hurt her, because of me, I beg you. I'd never forgive you if you did. Give all three of us time. I need it, so do you and Amanda."

"Yes, Susan, you're right. I shouldn't have said what I did."

"Please, please don't tell Amanda that I've told you her secret!" Susan pleaded.

"I won't, I promise. Only I wish in a way I hadn't been made to see the truth . . . fool that I am."

"Be gentle with her, Roger. Very gentle. She's a good girl and lucky will be the man who eventually wins her."

He held her hand very tightly.

"Because I love you, I'll keep my promises."

Susan rose.

"Come on. I think it's high time we went home."

They stared at each other and then broke into spontaneous laughter. With it, and the breeze from the sea, the embarrassment at the revelation of secrets vanished completely.

CHAPTER FOURTEEN

From that day on, Roger was very careful not to go out alone with Susan, or to call too often at the cottage. She understood his motives and praised him secretly for his determination, yet she missed his gay company. He seemed to sense when Amanda was with Susan, for it was on these occasions that he would visit her and Tony.

The summer came in with a blast of heat which lasted for three whole weeks. The turf on the cliffs grew brown and crackled as the sun baked it. The sea was calm and sparkled with a cobalt blue; a brilliant, peaceful and bottomless expanse of water. The village was inundated with visitors as the holiday season started up again with a swing. The villagers were both flabbergasted and pleased with the number of their visitors.

"There seem to be more this year than ever before!" Amanda's mother declared as she toiled in the kitchen. Both she and Amanda were being over-

worked, and because Mrs. Porter had had a bad attack
of bronchitis during the winter, Roger insisted that
she should on no account overtax herself. Susan suggested she should help out instead.

"Oh Sue, would you really?" Amanda cried delightedly. "Do you think you can manage?"

"Of course."

"What about Tony?"

"He'll be all right in his pram in the back garden
during the mornings while we're cooking. If I can find
someone to mind him after lunch until we close at
six, it'd be a great help. He can't be expected to lie in
his pram alone all day long. He must have someone
to take him out and play with."

In the middle of June, when trade was beginning to
get hectic, Susan joined the staff of the "Honeypot"
By this time Tony had become a very active young
man, and was taking a great deal of notice of what
went on around him. Mrs. Martin, who owned the
grocer's shop at the end of the main street, was
willing to care for him each afternoon until her
daughter, Fiona, came home from school at five,
when she took over the task of baby-minding. Mrs.
Martin assured Susan that Fiona would be only too
delighted to take full charge once the summer holidays started in late July.

Susan enjoyed her new life. She rose very early in
the mornings in order to get all her own chores done
before wheeling Tony down to the tea-shop at nine
o'clock. The baby had his morning nap in the small
garden while Susan and Amanda prepared the dining-
room and did the baking for the day's customers. Mrs.
Porter did very little in the kitchen, although she was

kept busy in the tea-room. When they were open, she sat in a corner at the till while Susan waited at table.

June and July came and went, and August was upon them. Business had never been busier, the two girls being almost rushed off their feet. Teas were served between three and six, but even these hours were filled to capacity, to say nothing of the hours of preparation that went on beforehand. The shop was rarely empty of customers. Susan quickly realized why Amanda had decided not to serve lunches. There would never have been any free time at all for either girl, with the tea-shop filled for many long hours daily. The dining-room itself was as full as they could allow. Fourteen tables, with four chairs at each, had been packed into the room, leaving just sufficient space for Mrs. Porter's cash desk and room for the girls to pass the customers as they ate.

Amanda's specialties were lobster — and cream teas. The lobsters were purchased from the fishermen on the quay, and all the fancy cakes and dainties were homemade.

The weather continued fine until the end of the second week in August when it broke suddenly in a tremendous thunderstorm. Afterwards, the heat lessened and dull, drizzling days took over from fine, sun-filled ones. The drizzle fell day after day, which gave the two girls a well-earned breathing space because the number of holidaymakers slackened off considerably. It was only the spartan few who braved the weather in mackintoshes and armed with umbrellas to trudge through the rain-soaked village.

It was now one of these afternoons late in August. One couple remained sipping tea and smoking ciga-

rettes as the clock hands crept towards six .. Mrs.
Porter had joined her daughter and Susan in the
kitchen where they were also drinking tea and finish-
ing some of the many cakes that were left over. Suddenly the bell on the front door tinkled. Amanda fast-
ened her eyes on the hatch

"Coming in or going?" Susan asked.

"They'd better not be leaving because they haven't
paid yet!" Mrs. Porter murmured.

Susan stood up, and smoothed down her pale green
nylon apron.

"I'll see to it."

"It's a man, and he's alone," Amanda told her
"He's gone to the window table "

Susan picked up her notepad and pushed the swing-
door leading into the dining-room. She saw that the
newcomer had taken the nearer of the two window
tables and was sitting with his back to her, looking
out onto the rain-soaked quay beyond. She went up
to him, pencil poised.

"Will you order, sir?" she asked.

The man turned and Susan thought she would
faint She went sheet-white and trembled violently

It was Glyn.

For a moment the world rocked dizzily before it
steadied again. Grey eyes held blue, with a depth of
unspoken misery and meaning. She could see that he
was just as shocked as she was. Masculine mouth
quivered as he struggled to find words which refused
to come, and the muscles of his left cheek worked
frantically.

Very slowly he rose, until he stood looking down
on her.

Susan gulped, longing to flee, but somehow her feet were stuck to the ground almost as if this was nothing more than a very bad dream.

"Sue! Oh, Sue!" he whispered, his voice thick with emotion.

The spell broken at last, Susan fled, fear lending her wings.

"I'm sorry," she gasped. "Someone else'll come." Then she stumbled into the kitchen, knocking over a chair as she went and oblivious of two pairs of interested eyes that watched her progress from the other table. Amanda jumped as Susan fell against the table, panting hard.

"Whatever's wrong?" she demanded, hurrying to her side.

"I can't tell you now, but I must go home ... please! At once!" Susan cried, distraught. Amanda made no move to stop her. Susan's eyes were blinded by tears as she ripped off her apron and reached for her mack. Without another word, she opened the door and ran away.

"Well!" Mrs. Porter declared. "Whatever's come over our Sue?"

"Leave this to me, Mother," Amanda advised as her mother started to move towards the tea-room. When she entered it, Glyn walked quickly towards her. She recognized his face but for the moment was unable to place it.

"My wife, where is she?" he demanded anxiously. "I must talk to her."

Of course! Glyn Moore. No wonder Susan had fled in such terror.

"May I come into your kitchen?" he persisted,

shepherding her expertly back to the door.

"This way," Amanda said. When the door had swung to behind them both, she went on, "Your wife's gone, Mr. Moore."

"Where? Tell me, where can I find her? Which way did she go?" Glyn was desperate and Amanda's heart went out to him. In the fleeting moment she had come face to face with this man, she had learned one important fact. He was as desperate for his wife as she was for him, although wild horses wouldn't permit her to admit it.

Amanda made up her mind. Susan and Glyn needed each other and must be forced to sort out their differences somehow, and she would help them as much as possible. She told him how to find Susan's cottage. He thanked her, went back into the tea-room for his coat, and then left. Amanda watched him from the swing-door, thinking grimly to herself.

Now try and get yourself out of this little muddle, Susan, my poor misguided friend!

CHAPTER FIFTEEN

How Susan reached home, she never knew. She stumbled through the puddles in the narrow, twisting streets, her head lowered to keep the incessant drizzle out of her eyes, and blundered into people Acquaintances turned to stare after her in amazement when she ignored their greetings. Thrusting the cottage key into the lock, she went inside and slammed the door. She then ran into the kitchen and sank down onto a chair, with her head on the table.

Why had Glyn come here today? What stroke of bad luck had directed his feet to this particular village, or had he known beforehand where to find her? She wanted to cry but shock had dried up all her tears, leaving her throat stiff and sore.

Would he follow her from the "Honeypot"? If so, what should she say to him? On the other hand, there was no reason for him to come up here to the cottage for he had made it perfectly clear he wanted nothing further to do with her.

The old ship's bell rang.

She stood up slowly, her hands cold and trembling. She must answer the door; it need not necessarily be Glyn outside. As she walked through the small hallway she knew without doubt whom she would find standing on the doorstep. Her hand hovered on the latch, and she wondered if she could thrust the bolt noiselessly, and pretend she was not in. He was a persistent person, and would only return later, so what was the point in postponing their meeting? Better to get it over and done with.

She lifted the latch and drew the door back carefully.

They stared at each other. Glyn's face was inscrutable although guarded. Her own lips were firm, willpower forcing her to stop their trembling.

"You'd better come in," she said at last.

"Thanks."

She led the way into the sitting-room and stood by the fireplace while Glyn went over to the large window, to look out.

"I should imagine that without this hovering sea mist, you get a magnificent view from here," he began conversationally, trying to break the ice.

"Yes. It is beautiful on a fine day."

There was a silence, then Glyn cleared his throat and turned to face he.

"It was pure chance that brought me to this village today."

"Oh?" She tried to sound disinterested.

"Yes. I've been spending a fortnight or so at St. Ives and decided to spend the last few days travelling home slowly to see the countryside as I went. Today I had the impulse to explore the coves and inlets along this part of the south coast. This place was to be my last port of call because I'm due back at work the day after tomorrow."

"So you work now, do you?" Susan's voice was scornful as she remembered past occasions when it had not mattered one iota to him whether he turned up at the office punctually or not. Glyn allowed the remark to pass. He went on:

"The weather's been so poor recently that I felt it was an excellent opportunity of seeing a few of the places one hasn't time for when the roads are crowded with holidaymakers. Most of the cars I passed were *en route* for the towns, and not the coast because of this drizzle."

"You came by car?"

"Yes. I'm permitted to drive again. My licence was suspended for a short time after ... after the accident. When I'd parked my car farther up the lane leading from the village, I walked around a bit and then saw the 'Honeypot' sign, which reminded me that I was very hungry."

"Another half an hour and you'd have been too late!" she declared fiercely. "We close at six."

"Then it was even more fortuitous I found the tea-shop in time. I think Fate must have brought me here and guided my steps towards you again." He moved to her but she turned away quickly. His voice was vibrant with a great sadness.

"I've had many months in which to think over what I quickly came to realize was over-hasty action. I've missed you, Sue."

"Have you?" She tried to make her tone disinterested. She did not trust Glyn, and was wondering exactly what game he was playing. Watch out for the Mohr cunning! a small voice urged although she longed to throw herself at him and tell him how much she had missed him too. Things were different now. She had pushed him out of her life, it must stay that way.

"Yes," he went on. "After you'd left, and I felt better, I sold that terrible house. Suddenly I began to see it as you had ... a monstrosity of bricks and mortar, not a home. I also sold all the furniture you'd hated so much. Then I bought a modern house. It's very much smaller, of course, but far easier to run. The tragedy is that it's exactly the kind of place you'd asked me to buy in the very beginning! I think it must have been the passage of time and living away from it that made me realize how appalling the other place was!" He smiled ruefully. "If only I'd done so before we were married then perhaps ...? But no," he added quickly, his voice firm and brisk. "It wouldn't have made any difference to us."

"So you're not living with your parents after all?" Susan's tone was bitterly sarcastic.

"No. I was mad even to have considered it. Believe me, Sue, it must have been that bang on the head. For months I couldn't bring myself to think coherently. I realize I must have been an extremely difficult person to deal with."

"No more so than before," Susan interrupted spitefully, then bit her lip. "I shouldn't have said that."

However, Glyn appeared completely unruffled.

"As soon as I'd recovered full use of this leg ...

and I don't even limp now   I decided to leave my parents. Naturally, there was an awful fuss, but you know, Susan, when you've lived with someone else away from your parents for even a short time, it's very, very difficult to go back to the mode of life you'd had previously. I didn't like being alone."

Susan made no reply. She too knew the meaning of loneliness! How dared he complain that *he* was lonely, almost as if he was blaming her for being responsible!

"How've you been keeping?" he asked, after an awkward pause.

"Quite well, thanks."

Glyn wandered about the room, inspecting the furnishings and knick-knacks. He looked at her, his mouth twisted in a sneer.

"I see you made excellent use of the money you took from Father."

"Please! You're being unfair."

"Am I? It was true, wasn't it? All along you'd deceived me. You hadn't wanted me, while I, like a fool, had flattered myself into thinking I could make you want me. And all the time it was money you were after!" he added bitterly. "I'll tell you something, Susan. There isn't a man on this earth who can stomach the knowledge that he's a failure with the woman he loves. Of course, most of it was my own stupid fault. I realize now how wrong and selfish I'd been. I blamed you for my failure with the unhappy result that I tried to hurt and bully you into loving me, thereby raising my own ego.

"You were right, of course. From the very beginning you were right! We were totally unsuited and should not have risked marriage. Now do you understand why I'm glad to have met you today. We can sit down and have a sane, unemotional discussion on where we can go from here. A separation is neither one thing nor the other, and is consequently useless to us both. I suggest we make a final, clean break."

"Divorce?"

"Naturally. What other course lies open?"

"I see." Susan paused, then asked: "Do you wish to remarry, is that it?"

"I've no one in mind at the moment, but it's quite possible both of us may want to marry someone else in the near future."

Susan looked down at her hands.

"I suppose it might happen ... one day," she said in a small voice, although she knew she would never want to.

"Can I rent a room in the village?" Glyn asked.

"There's an inn. I expect they'll have a free room."

"Good. Then I suggest I stay there tonight and we'll meet in the morning to discuss the matter of a divorce."

"It'll have to be very early. I start work at nine. I'm sure Amanda won't mind if I spare you an hour from nine till ten."

"You needn't worry about evidence, Susan. I'll provide it if you wish. Save you the embarrassment."

"Indeed? Surely such action on your part won't exactly meet with your parents' approval?" she enquired, her voice heavy with sarcasm. Glyn was about to protest when they both heard the front door open and Fiona's cheerful voice.

Tony!

Susan knew panic. She had forgotten time was passing so swiftly. What a fool she'd been to let Glyn into the cottage in the first place! If he should see Tony, or even find out about him, he'd know at once whose child he was because the baby was growing more and more like his father every day. What could she do?

Nothing. It was far, far too late.

Perhaps Fiona would take Tony straight upstairs, then Glyn could be whisked out of the house before he found out.

In the hallway Fiona chattered to Tony, and the child laughed gaily. Glyn frowned suddenly, and looked searchingly at Susan who was standing in the middle of the room, her hand at her throat, and a terrified expression on her face

Then the worst happened. Fiona opened the door and came in, carrying Tony. She caught sight of Glyn, and stopped, confused

"I'm sorry, Mrs. Moore. I didn't realize you had a guest. I'll take Tony straight upstairs, shall I? I can stay to put him to bed, if you'd like me to."

"Yes. Yes, please, Fiona," Susan replied wildly The girl turned to leave the room but it was now that Tony asserted his own authority. He suddenly decided he wanted his mother. His face wrinkled with disgust and he thrust out both arms, crying:

"Mmmmmmumumum!"

Fiona smiled and patted his back gently. She carried him over to Susan

"I'm sorry, Mrs. Moore, it seems he wants you for a moment before I take him up to bed. There you are, my poppet, Mummy'll have you."

Tony burbled and bounced delightedly, clinging onto Susan's neck and dribbling down her cheek. Then he turned to beam at Glyn.

Susan was watching her husband's reaction, and she saw the unmistakable signs of strain and shock. He gripped the back of the armchair until his knuckles stood out very white. His eyes were bleak and his mouth quivered. Then he blinked rapidly four or five times . . .

"Thank you for bringing him home, Fiona. You needn't stay now. I'll put him to bed."

"That's all right, Mrs. Moore. You know I love doing anything for this gorgeous little man!" Fiona came over to Susan and kissed Tony's chubby cheek. She turned to Glyn and smiled; "He's a beautiful baby, isn't he, sir?"

Glyn's mouth had steadied into a hard, white line, but he managed to nod to Fiona before she left.

Susan decided to forestall his comments.

"Glyn, Tony's *our* son," she said shakily. Glyn flinched and came over to her, put his hand under the baby's chin and turned his head fully towards him. Naturally, Tony resented this high-handed treatment. He pursed up his mouth and began to cry before cringing back to the safety of Susan's neck. From then on, he kept casting suspicious glances at his father.

"Now you've frightened him!" Susan scolded Glyn.

"If I'd had any doubts when the girl brought the baby in just now, they've been dispelled. I've only had to look at him closely to see he's indeed my own

son. He even has my coloring!'' he declared angrily as
if it was a personal affront. Susan could not help a
smile.

"Children have a habit of taking after their parents, you know. Tony's always been more like you
than me, ever since he was born.''

"And when was that?'' Glyn demanded.

"I ... oh, I see what you mean. Tony arrived on
January 22nd.''

Glyn looked at her quickly and she could see him
doing some rapid mental calculations.

"Then ... and you say he's my child ... yet how
can he be?'' he murmured. "Unless ... unless,'' he
paced the room, frowning so hard that the devil's
eyebrows met and blended. Suddenly he looked at
her. "It must have been sometime near the accident.
It could only be then ... it must have been! It's
impossible, because we hadn't been sharing beds for
months before the car smash.'' He resumed his pac-
ing, while Susan watched him.

"Sue, I don't quite know how to say this, but has
Tony anything to do with our quarrel? I realize I
ought to know but I don't! Confound it, Susan, those
lost hours are still quite blank. You must tell me! Did
I force you to make love to me a short time before the
accident? Did I? Tell me, *did* I?'' He had raised his
voice and Tony started whimpering again.

"Yes, yes, yes!'' Susan yelled back at him. "But
it's of no importance now. I have Tony, and until you
came here today we were both happy. Now please go,
Glyn. I want to put him to bed. I can't speak to you
tonight. Oh, please, please ... *go*!'' Her own eyes
were full of tears, and the baby was clinging so tightly

around her neck that she was almost choking.

Glyn swallowed hard.

"Very well, Susan, I'll leave. I hope you realize what a tremendous shock this has been to me, but we'll talk about it in the morning ... early."

"Yes, yes. In the morning. We'll thrash it out tomorrow."

CHAPTER SIXTEEN

Susan hardly slept at all that night. Her encounter with Glyn had been so completely unexpected; she felt as though she had stepped heedlessly into a quagmire and was now sinking slowly. Glyn had made it abundantly clear that he wanted a divorce. Almost from the moment he had stepped inside the cottage she had known he had not come to ask her to return to him, but now there was another, far more terrible dread in her mind. Until today he had been in ignorance about the baby. Unfortunately, since he now knew Tony existed, and was his own son, it was impossible not to believe he would try to take him away from her.

She spent hours tossing and turning on her bed, wondering. Then common sense reasserted itself to remind her that a very young baby's place was with its mother.

What about the proposed divorce? Would Glyn now try to win custody of Tony so that his son would be brought up in the way he stipulated? If this was the plan, then she was prepared to fight him tooth and nail to keep her child.

Just before dark that evening, Amanda had called at the cottage.

"I know Mr. Moore has gone," she began. "I saw him go into the inn. May I come in?"

"Of course." Wearily Susan held the door for her friend.

"Please don't think I'm being nosy, but I felt you might like someone to talk to after the sudden encounter with your husband."

"Yes. Yes, I must talk to you," Susan had agreed and together the two girls had sat long into the night talking. Amanda commented little, until she had asked:

"What are you going to do?"

"I just don't know! I suppose I'd better wait until the morning to hear what Glyn's proposing. Oh, how I *wish* he hadn't seen Tony!"

"He'd have found out sometime, you know, Sue," Amanda told her tactfully. "I know everything looks very bad at the moment, but something's bound to turn up."

"You don't know Glyn!" Susan had wailed miserably.

"No, I don't. From the little I've seen of him, I didn't get the impression he was planning to hurt you. Far from it."

"Really? Which all goes to show how little you *do* know about him! I've been tricked in the past, and I'm not going to allow him to get his own way ever again. Especially where Tony's concerned."

"Go to bed, Sue, you look absolutely worn out. Shall I get you anything before I leave?"

Susan had declined.

"Then I'll leave you to your thoughts."

"I might be a little late at the shop in the morning, if that's all right with you?"

"You come along whenever you and Glyn have finished your discussion. Mother and I can cope for a few hours." Amanda had gone to the door to let herself out, then she turned to say: "Oh, Sue, I've a suggestion. Wouldn't it be easier if I came up here about half past eight and took Tony off your hands? Then his presence won't be an added distraction while you're with your husband."

"Would you? That *is* a load off my mind."

Early the following morning Susan began to tidy away as much evidence of Tony's occupation as she could find. His bricks and toys she put out of sight in a cupboard, the mending was pushed into a corner of the bedroom instead of being left in its usual pile on the table beside her armchair. The only item she was obliged to leave was a clothes-line of diapers fluttering in the breeze outside the back door, but men never noticed that kind of thing.

Amanda arrived to collect Tony in his pram at twenty-five past eight, after which Susan sat down to wait for Glyn. She picked up a book to pass the time but her eyes were forever straying towards the clock.

Why, oh why did time drag so?

After what seemed hours of impatient waiting, Glyn eventually arrived a few minutes past nine o'clock. Once inside the cottage he looked round hopefully, then scowled.

"Where's my son?" he demanded, his voice arrogant.

"With friends. I thought it better we should be alone while discussing our matrimonial problem. Glyn, I haven't much time, so I'd be grateful if we got straight down to business. I ought really to be at work by now."

"I see. By the way, one small but very important point. What happens to our child while you work?"

Susan explained the arrangements she had made.

"Do you honestly think it's a good idea?" he asked.

"Yes. I'm helping Amanda and her mother who have been very good to me ever since I arrived here last year. At the same time I'm earning a small wage. Tony's also well cared for. He sleeps in his pram most of the morning, a thing he'd do in any case, whether I went to work or not, and then he has the company of other young children after I've given him his dinner. Fiona's brother and sisters love Tony and are very good for him, I'm certain."

"What of the future? Do you intend to continue living in this way?"

"For a while, yes. The summer season ends soon, then I'll be free to be with Tony all the time. Next summer, of course, he'll be very much more active and walking. He'll be able to play with the other village children by then. As soon as he's old enough to go to the local primary school, I'll be able to think about getting some other kind of job."

"I understand." Suddenly he swung round on her and snapped, "Why the hell didn't you tell me you were pregnant?" Susan jumped, then reminded him:

"I tried to, Glyn. I wanted to come and tell you in person if you think back, only your father refused to allow me near his house. He told me that *you* couldn't be bothered with me any more," she added, the scorn in her voice cutting him like a knife. "After that I knew how useless it was to go on trying to tell you. I thought I'd probably be able to struggle along on my own somehow or other, then your father offered me a large sum of money."

"Which you accepted without any hesitation whatsoever, so he informed me!" Glyn's voice was hard and bitter. Susan's eyes widened.

"But of course! It was the most natural thing to do, to take that money. Don't you understand? It came as the answer to all my worries, therefore I was able to take it without any qualms of conscience because I meant to use it solely for the baby. I invested most of it and have managed to live reasonably well, as long as I go carefully, on the small income it's brought me."

"You had money in your own banking account! The account I opened for you when we were married. Why didn't you use that as well?"

"I did."

"Only to send regular monthly gifts to your mother." Susan turned from him. "Oh yes, Sue, I know all about it. I had a heated argument with the bank manager and, in the end, he grudgingly told me what I needed to know about your money. I wanted to give you more, and I even tried to reach you through him, but he refused to tell me where he thought you must have gone."

"Under my instructions, naturally, although I was

careful not to tell him exactly where I was going to live. Still, he might have guessed to within a radius of ten miles or so.''

"Why didn't you use the money I gave you?" Glyn demanded angrily. "Why continue to give it to your mother when your own need was greater? Damn it all, you're my wife and have the right to sufficient money for our child!''

"I didn't think so. I didn't want to touch any money that came from you.''

"I was bitterly shocked on learning you hadn't touched a penny for yourself," he stated unhappily.

Susan swung away from the mantelpiece and crossed to the chair nearest him where she stood looking down at him as he sat on the settee.

"Of course you were shocked ... but only because on discovering that I *wasn't* using it, you had the uneasy feeling that perhaps I hadn't married you for your money after all! I had my pride, Glyn. I wasn't going to be dependent on you any longer.''

"A damned silly kind of pride, I must say!" he snapped angrily. "I'm your husband and you'd a right to that money.''

"As I'd a right to everything else of yours, including your companionship and a share of your household, perhaps?" Susan jeered.

Glyn lowered his gaze, ashamed.

"I'm sorry, Sue. I did wrong. I acted too hastily in accepting my parents' offer of care. I ought to have thought more of you and less of myself.''

"You may be apologetic now, but you were perfectly clear-headed and adamant when you made your original decision not to come home to me.

Anyway, where the money was concerned, I felt your father owed me every penny he offered ... and more ... He had set out to drive a wedge between us, and he'd succeeded very well indeed. Beyond his wildest hopes and dreams, in fact." Susan raised her chin determinedly.

"Oh yes, Glyn Mohr, I'd have taken all of your father's fortune, had he offered it, yet your own money I wouldn't have touched. Wild horses couldn't have made me! I had to keep up my small contribution to my Mother, though."

"What a strange girl you are!"

"No, I'm not. It's quite possible I prefer to stretch the pennies rather than be censured by Mother."

"Sue, I saw her a few months ago," Glyn said slowly.

"Oh? How ... how was she?"

"Quite well, and very sorry to have received your letter."

"Did ... did she say anything to you about it?" Susan asked with reluctance. Glyn looked at her thoughtfully.

"As a matter of fact, she did. She said that when I found you I was to tell you that until you could learn to love your husband as you should ... as she had told you ... then she'd rather you didn't come to see her again." Susan turned away, biting her lip. "I'm sorry, my dear, but she wasn't too pleased with *either* of us! As a matter of fact, I rather threw myself at her mercy, begging her to tell me where I could find you. But she didn't know."

Susan's hands began to shake and she had to clasp them firmly together. "Yes, my dear, hasn't it occurred to you that I might have wanted to find you in order to sort out our affairs?"

"No. I'm afraid I never thought of it like that."

Glyn continued more cheerfully.

"Yet your poor mother knew as little as I did."

Susan suddenly laughed.

"After all the elaborate precautions I took to keep our paths separate! I needn't have bothered, need I? Fate steps in and plays her dirty trick by showing you exactly where to find me. Bang! Just like that. Oh, cruel, cruel Destiny. Why, oh why did you have to come here?" she cried, her voice harsh and bitter.

There was a long pause before Glyn said:

"Yesterday, when we met, I told you I wanted to discuss divorce. At the time I was unaware I had a son."

"What difference does it make to the divorce?" Susan demanded hastily, fear pounding in her chest. "You can't take him away from me, because I won't let you! Anyway, the Court would never allow such a thing."

"Susan! Will you *please* let me finish what I'd started to say? Yesterday I didn't know about Tony, but today I see that divorce is completely out of the question."

Susan's heart leapt uncontrollably. What was he getting at now? "Why?" she asked, guardedly.

Glyn looked at her, his expression unfathomable.

"It's out of the question because I want my son. I'm not going to allow you to have sole charge of him," he added firmly.

Susan gasped with horror.

"I ... I," she began, then stopped, at a loss for words.

"All night I've lain awake thinking about you and the baby. Fortunately I came to this conclusion. For all our sakes, but mainly for the child's, I want you to leave here and come home with me. Back to my new house where Tony can be raised by both his parents guiding and caring for him."

"How strange you should say such a thing!" she mused almost to herself. "Someone else used almost the same argument to me not so very long ago. I mean, where Tony and I are concerned ... Tony needing a father as well as a mother."

"Who said it?" Glyn demanded, suspicion on his face.

"A friend ... a very dear friend," Susan replied haughtily.

"Male?"

Susan did not reply.

"I see." Glyn cleared his throat. "I've made my proposition. I'm asking you to come back with me so we may live together again and have the enjoyment of bringing up our own child."

Susan threw back her head and laughed gaily. Glyn lurched towards her, grabbed her arms and shook her hard.

"Stop it! Stop it at once! You're hysterical."

"I'm not. I'm just highly amused." Carefully she removed his restraining hands and moved away from him, all laughter gone. "You're so two-faced! Less than eighteen hours ago, you stood in this very room telling me in detail why you thought we should get divorced. This morning, however, we've a complete change of tune, and all because you've discovered you'd been a father for seven months. Today you're asking me to come and live with you again.'' She went over to him, demanding angrily:

''What do you think I am? I'm not prepared to make the same mistake twice, even if you are. As you so very, very kindly explained yesterday, we just don't belong together, and I'm really interested in your wealth. Face the truth, Glyn. You don't want *me*! You feel you have to ask me because I'm the commodity which comes with the baby, but he's the only one you really want, isn't he? Let me say one thing, Glyn Mohr, for seven months Tony and I've got on extremely well, each needing the other, and no one else. We've sufficient money to keep us, as long as I'm careful. We've made our lives in this village, and are happy in them. Why, I've even altered the spelling of our surname to get away from my memories! M-O-O-R-E. Don't disrupt everything now, please! For many reasons, most of them too complicated and personal to explain at the moment, I just don't want to go back with you. I'm used to living here and I'm set in my ways because I like living here. So please go away and leave us alone, will you? Tony's still a baby. We shall not run away, I promise, but let's go ahead with the divorce as you suggested yesterday. You wanted it, you said so. I expect the Court will allow you reasonable access to Tony.''

''I want my child all the time!'' Glyn stated harshly.

''Oh no, that I can't permit. You'd have to fight me in court before I allowed you to take him away from me.'' She touched his arm, her voice now gentle. ''Be reasonable, Glyn. There's still over a year to run before you can sue me for desertion. Get your divorce then, I won't try to stop you, although I'll fight to keep Tony." Her eyes were alight with the fire of battle. "He's my baby and no one, not even you, shall take him from me! I certainly don't want to live with you again, so you can forget that idea. It'd be inflicting utter misery on both of us because you told me *it wouldn't work*."

"Yesterday I thought differently," he mumbled.

"Nothing important's changed. How could it?" Susan gripped Glyn's arm fiercely. She felt tongues of fire sweep upward as she touched his firm muscles beneath the coat sleeve. If she gave in now all would be lost.

"Glyn, please, please leave us alone!" she implored.

"Very well, Susan, I know when I'm beaten. I'll do as you wish. I'll not force you to come with me."

Suddenly he smiled.

"Don't look so scared, Sue. I'll not hurt you or him, but I want you to promise not to refuse me permission to see Tony should I come back to the village any time. Just before I go, may I see Tony?" he asked gently.

"Yes, Glyn. I can't prevent you seeing Tony if you're here. But how often will that be? You have your work in town. Or are you..." she stopped.

"I knew you probably wouldn't believe me if I told you but I now work regular hours each week, Monday to Saturday. Quite a surprise, isn't it?

"After the accident I learned many home truths, one of them resulting in my decision to earn a salary by honest, hard work. Secondly, I've forsaken all forms of alcohol ..."

"But you weren't drunk that night! I don't care what they said, you were *not* drunk ..."

"Whether I was or not, I've taken a distinct disliking for the stuff. Many's the occasion in the past when I *have* come very near to one too many, whatever you say. In the meantime, you'll oblige me by accepting a cheque."

"I ... I," she began, then shut her mouth. Glyn unscrewed his gold fountain-pen looking at her wistfully.

"I'll not insult you by giving you money, but please take this as a gift for Tony."

"Not ... not too much," she begged.

"Here are my home and office telephone numbers, in case you need them."

"I doubt it."

"Sue! I know you distrust me, and I can't say I blame you. However, I want you to have this. Of course, you may never need to ring me, but if Tony should be ill, or you yourself need something urgently, then you can call on me at once."

Susan pouted.

"As Tony's father I have a right to be told immediately if anything's wrong," Glyn declared angrily. They walked down the hill into the village in silence. Neighbors nodded greetings and stared with interest at Glyn.

"Do you know everyone?" he asked, smiling.

"Most of them. Here we are." Susan opened the gate into the garden behind the "Honeypot". Tony lay in his pram, fast asleep. Glyn bent over him, the eagerness leaving his face and keen disappointment taking its place.

"I won't stay, Sue. I mustn't wake him now, must I?" He stared down at the angelic sleeping face with its golden wisps of hairs, and a slow delighted smile lightened his expression. Susan saw the gentle wistfulness and her heart quivered.

Glyn broke the silence.

"Goodbye, Susan." he said and turned away from the pram. "I'll let you know in good time when I'll next be in the village. I don't expect I can make it before three weeks."

He hurried away. Susan stayed to watch him, hoping he would turn back to wave, but he did not do so Then she went into the kitchen where Amanda and her mother were waiting, their faces eager.

"Well?" said Amanda. "We saw you through the window, deep in conversation. What's been decided?"

"Amanda!" her mother remonstrated.

Susan smiled, knowing neither would be satisfied until they had been told what she and Glyn had decided.

"He doesn't want a divorce, not now he knows about Tony," she explained. "He asked me to go back to him, but only for Tony's sake."

"You agreed, naturally," Amanda commented.

"Goodness, no! Why should I?"

"Because you love him, of course."

Susan blushed furiously.

"That has nothing to do with it. I admit I do love him, but he mustn't ever know because he plainly doesn't want me. He told me so yesterday when we talked of divorce."

"What other plan has he?"

"Nothing at the moment, or so he said. He wants to see the baby again and I've agreed."

Amanda regarded her friend with one eyebrow raised.

"All right, then, you tell me, Amanda! How can I stop Glyn seeing Tony?" Susan demanded.

The other girl wagged a floury finger at her.

"Surely this is the point, do you really want to stop him?"

Susan shuffled her feet.

"No. No, of course not. All I want is for Glyn to find out that he wants me just as much, if not more, than he wants Tony. But at the moment," she finished sadly, "I figure very little in his thoughts."

"Huh!" Amanda scoffed.

"What do you mean ... 'huh!'?"

"Nothing. Just huh!"

CHAPTER SEVENTEEN

Susan did not return to the "Honeypot" for four days.

Tony was by no means his usual smiling self. He was teasy and fretful, and dribbled a great deal.

Susan suggested to Fiona that she go up to the cottage to look after Tony for a couple of days rather than allow the child to spread his cold germs around the rest of her family. Fiona agreed and called at the tea-shop to collect the pram after lunch. Before she left, Susan promised to be home as early as she could that evening.

Unfortunately, luck was against her that Wednesday. At five o'clock a coachload of trippers arrived on their doorstep, demanding tea.

Susan was kept busy hurrying in and out of the kitchen with dirty crockery and fresh plates piled high with cakes and buns and teapots that always seemed to need replenishing. It was with considerable surprise, therefore, that she saw the back door open and

Fiona rush into the kitchen, panting hard. Alarm filled her.

"Mrs. Moore ... come quickly! Oh, please come quickly!" she cried, tugging at Susan's arm. Two cups fell off the tray to shatter on the floor as Susan slammed it down on the table. Amanda's mother turned from the sink where she was washing dishes and stared at the distraught young girl.

"What's happened?" Susan gasped. "Tony! Where is he?"

"They're taking him away. Oh, please let's be quick before it's too late.

"I tried to stop them. I said he'd just had a bad cold and was going to bed, but they wouldn't listen. The woman dressed him again after I'd finished the bath. They said they were his grandparents, and that they'd come to take him back to his rightful home."

Susan stopped dead.

"Fiona! The cottage!" she called. When she reached the garden she saw the front door standing open. She dashed inside shouting Tony's name. The pram in the hall stood empty. Even the rugs and blankets were missing. She went into the lounge and stared down at the floor. The playpen stood as Fiona had left it when she had taken Tony up for his bath. Bricks lay higgledy-piggledy on the carpet while Tony's teddy bear rested face down under the table. She ran upstairs to look into the bathroom and Tony's bedroom, both of which were empty. She came down again and went into the lounge. Then she dropped onto the settee.

Fiona joined her. She was crying bitterly.

"I'd just brought him down from the bathroom in

his dressing-gown and sleeping suit. We were playing together on the floor when ... they came. I opened the front door, then that ... that awful woman marched right in and demanded to know where the baby was." She gripped Susan's arm.

"Oh, I tried to stop them, really I did, but I didn't know whether I ought to stay with Tony or come straight for you."

Susan drew the girl close and folded her arms around her, holding her tightly.

"There, there, my dear, you did all you could. You were very brave and sensible. It wasn't your fault at all. I ought to have guessed something like this would happen."

"You'll never forgive me!" Fiona wailed.

"There's nothing to forgive. I know you did everything in your power to protect Tony. I know both the persons concerned, and I think you stood up to them marvellously."

Fiona caught sight of the teddy bear under the table. She bent down to pick it up. Then she gave it to Susan.

"Look, they've left his little teddy! He'll be miserable without it."

Susan held the toy to her cheek. At that moment there was a screeching of brakes outside the cottage. Susan's heart leapt. Was it possible her in-laws had had a change of heart and were now returning?

Together they dashed out into the hall and Fiona pulled open the front door. It was Roger. Fiona hung onto his arm and poured out an incoherent tale. His face was grim. He went at once to Susan and put his arm round her, leading her back to the settee. She leaned against him, weeping.

"Amanda phoned me and told me to get up here at once. What's all this Fiona's been saying about young Tony?"

Through her sobs Susan began the story. Throughout it all, Roger smoothed her hair gently.

"There, darling!" he murmured.

"Oh, Roger, I trusted Glyn!" she wailed reproachfully. "Fool that I was, I should have known better. He never did allow anything to stand in the way of what he wanted."

"Calm yourself, Sue. We'll get Tony back. His place is with you, his mother. Now, tell me, is there any way in which you can contact Glyn?"

"Yes! He made me take his phone numbers."

"Splendid." Roger stood up and helped her to her feet. Then he put his other arm round Fiona and gave her a comforting hug. "I'll drive you straight down to my place where you shall ring him. The sooner you two talk the better."

In Roger's cottage, Roger dialled the exchange and asked for the number of Glyn's office.

"I hope he hasn't gone home yet!" Susan murmured, wringing her hands anxiously.

"Mr. Moore please!" Roger snapped. "Mrs. Moore ... it's urgent ... Well, find him girl!"

Almost immediately Glyn was on the line. Silently Susan took the receiver from Roger.

"Susan, is something wrong?"

"You know there is. Glyn, I want Tony back ... tonight," she demanded fiercely.

"I'm sorry. I'm not with you. What do you mean?"

Her voice rose hysterically.

"You know right well what I mean. You're to bring Tony home at once."

"I'm awfully sorry, Sue, dear, but I honestly don't get it. Want Tony back ... why? Is he ill, or something?"

She stamped her foot impatiently.

"Stop fooling, Glyn," she hissed. "You needn't pretend with me. I know quite well you used your parents to come and take Tony away from me."

There was a sudden, shocked pause. She heard Glyn gasp. Then he said in a voice of ice:

"Tell my parents to take Tony away from you? Of course not, stupid!" He was now furiously, blindly, angry, and Susan quivered as he spat the words at her. "Haven't I given you my promise that I wouldn't ask for Tony just yet? I think you'd better be more explicit."

She began to cry bitterly.

"Then ... then it's nothing to do with you at all?" Her voice faltered. Roger took the receiver from her and said:

"Mr. Moore. This is Dr. Harlow, Susan's practitioner. Less than half an hour ago, a man and a woman, whom Susan assured me are your own parents, forced their way into Susan's home, terrified the young girl whom Susan had left in charge of her baby, and took the child away with them. The babysitter did her very best to dissuade your parents but they overruled her ... rudely, too, it would appear. She rushed to fetch your wife, but by the time they got back to the cottage, your parents had left ... with the baby."

Susan could hear the angry exclamation and torrent

of words on the other end of the line.

"I might also add, Mr. Moore, that the child has been under my care recently, and I consider it extremely inadvisable to have taken him out in a car at the present time. I cannot stress strongly enough how vital it is for Tony to be returned with all speed to his mother."

Glyn now spoke at length.

"Yes ... yes, Mr. Moore ... I'll do that ... very well ... then we'll leave it entirely in your hands .. Thank you." Roger put the receiver back into Susan's hands, and she listened eagerly.

"Sue, you're not to worry, understand?" Glyn said. "Your doctor will look after you until I arrive later tonight. You're not to do anything until I'm with you."

CHAPTER EIGHTEEN

Roger took Susan back to the cottage where he made her a cup of tea and gave her a sedative. Outside the gate, the police constable waited, while eager faces in the neighboring cottages watched the comings and goings.

"Good evening, sir. Anything I can do for the lady."

"No thank you, Frank. Everything's well under control."

"Ay. So the County Office told me. Seems the gentleman's called on us to stop the car. I expect they'll catch it at the Tamar Bridge."

The hours passed slowly. Amanda did her knitting while Susan lay staring up at the ceiling, saying nothing. The sun set and it became dark. Shortly after twelve, they heard a car coming up the road.

"Is it ...?" she faltered, her hand at her throat. Her knees were shaking. She felt too weak to move.

"I can't quite make it out," said Amanda peering

out into the darkness, "but I think it's your husband." She saw him open the rear door, lean inside and pick up a large bundle, wrapped in rugs. She turned a radiant face to Susan.

"Sue! He's got Tony!"

With wings on her feet, Susan rushed out into the hall and threw open the front door. Then she dashed down the garden path to meet Glyn.

"Tony! Tony!" she cried joyfully. They met, but Susan had eyes only for her child.

"Careful, he's fast asleep," Glyn warned. "Completely worn out, the poor little fellow." Then he placed the sleeping baby into his wife's open arms.

"He's safe, oh, he's safe! My darling baby." She pressed her cheek softly against the sleeping child.

Amanda came out, put her arm round Susan's waist and led her back to the cottage, followed by Glyn.

"Sue, darling, hadn't you better put him straight to bed?" she advised.

Tony stirred, opened his eyes and began to wail. He blinked up at Susan then recognized her. This seemed to reassure him completely, for he turned away at once and promptly went to sleep again.

Glyn touched her shoulder.

"Your friend's right, dear. Tony ought to be in bed."

Susan looked at him for the first time since he had given her back her child. Until that moment it had been as if he hadn't existed. Now she was filled with a surge of compassion for her neglect.

"Oh, Glyn, how can I ever thank you?" she murmured.

"We'll discuss that later," he said, and put his hand under her arm to guide her to the narrow staircase.

Amanda disappeared into the kitchen. A minute later there was a knock at the front door. She hurried to open it, admitting Roger.

"The child's home?"

"Yes. Upstairs with Sue."

"In that case I'd rather make sure he's all right before she tucks him in."

He took the stairs two at a time and went into Tony's room. She smiled gaily at him.

"Just a quick check before you finish," he said, pulling out his stethoscope. He made a rapid examination, then nodded. "No harm's been done, as far as I can tell. However, I'll pop in and see him first thing in the morning."

Roger joined the other two in the lounge. Glyn looked up hopefully as he entered the room.

"Your son's none the worse for his adventure," Roger told him.

"Thank heaven!"

"Mr. Mohr, naturally you won't be driving back to town at once will you? May my mother and I offer you a bed for the rest of the night? The inn's closed at this hour. They'll all have gone to bed ages ago."

"That's very kind of you, Miss Porter."

"Amanda, please."

"Amanda. I'll gladly accept your offer. I was a little worried because naturally Sue doesn't want me here. Are you quite sure I won't be causing you any inconvenience?"

Amanda reassured him and Susan entered the

room, her face radiating her joy. She was handed a cup of tea which Roger had liberally sugared beforehand.

"Ugh!" she said, grimacing. "Far too sweet."

"Drink it up," Roger ordered. Glyn looked at him and caught the gentle expression of love. So that was it! The doctor was the man Susan loved.

"Now please tell us, how did you find Tony?" Susan asked Glyn.

"As soon as you'd rung off, I rang the police. I realized they'd be the only ones with authority to halt my parent's car. I soon learned that the car had been stopped on the Tamar Bridge. Arriving there, I found Father ranting and raging and Mother hysterical." He scowled. "By the time I'd finished what I had to say to them, they were even more displeased. I want you to understand, Sue, before we go any further, that I'd no idea whatsoever of their plans. When I arrived home after seeing you recently, I was too pleased with the knowledge that I was a father to worry over their reactions. Both of them did their utmost to persuade me to come back here and remove Tony from your care. I refused, explaining that what you and I did was entirely up to us and no one else. I've very little doubt that my father's fertile brain hatched today's plot. And Mother simply cannot see that they'd done wrong! She only wanted to surprise me, by giving me back my son. Even though I argued and argued, she refuses to see it from your point of view. Tony is my child and, according to her, he should be living either in my house or in hers, with a nanny to care for him."

"They've now driven off home in a fearful huff. I

simply cannot understand my mother! How on earth she thought I'd care for a child while I'm at work all day, I don't know! Anyway, it's over now. I'm master in my own home, and intend it to stay that way. What I decide to do with my own son is my business . . . and yours too, my dear.'' He smiled at Susan and squeezed her hand quickly. She looked at him searchingly while Amanda glanced at Roger who was showing signs of jealousy. She stepped in at once.

"Sue, I've already told Glyn he can have a bed at the 'Honeypot'.''

"Thanks, Amanda.''

"I'll drive you home,'' Roger murmured while Amanda turned to Glyn.

"I'll leave with you, I expect poor Sue's dead tired and wants to go to bed after such a worrying evening.'' He went over to Susan who was now standing at the table, collecting cups and putting them on the tea-tray. "Sleep well, my dear. I'm quite sure Tony'll be none the worse for his outing.''

"What can I say, Glyn, except . . . thank you, from the bottom of my heart.'' He took her hands and held them very tightly. His voice was slightly husky.

"Nonsense! I'll call early in the morning. It'll have to be before nine, I'm afraid.''

"Do you . . . do you have to return so soon?'' Susan asked, with a twinge of disappointment.

"Yes. I'm sorry, but there's nothing I can do about it . . . much as I'd like to,'' he added softly.

Glyn's car arrived outside the cottage just after eight. He followed Susan into the kitchen where she was in the middle of giving Tony his breakfast.

"Do you mind helping Tony while I work around?

Take care, though, he has a horrid habit of upending the cup when my back's turned. I'll make the tea.''

Glyn sat down beside Tony who watched him thoughtfully. Suddenly he gurgled and smiled sunnily. Then he thrust a sodden biscuit straight into his father's eye. Susan laughed.

"You're now his friend for life!"

"I'm glad. What about you?" he went on looking at her. She turned away, confused, and fussed with the kettle.

"Sue, I want to talk to you. The milk's gone and he seems to have finished eating. Shall I put him in his playpen for a few minutes?"

"Please."

She sat at the table and poured out a second cup of tea.

"You might as well drink it while we talk," she said, replenishing her own.

"Sue, first of all, I promise that there'll never, never be a recurrence of yesterday's pantomime. We needn't worry about my parents. I'm certain they won't dare interfere again. As I told you when we met, I am prepared to wait, but since yesterday my opinions have changed. We'll have to make up our minds one way or the other sooner than agreed. This is my plan. I'll take a leave of absence for about ten days, depending on how work goes. I intend staying here in the village ... at the inn," he added pointedly as her eyes widened apprehensively.

"During this time I suggest we see as much of each other as we can, so that we may decide for certain whether there's any possibility of our living together again.

"We must try to see the problem from the other's angle. At the end of my visit, I'm confident we'll have had sufficient time to make up our minds.

"And I give you my word of honor now, Sue, that if you still find you can't bear the thought of coming back to live with me again, then I'll go away ... for good. I'll make no more claims on Tony ... and I'll also provide the necessary evidence so that you may divorce me. That's a fair bargain, isn't it?"

"Oh, Glyn!" her voice was sorrowful.

"Yes, it'll be a wrench for me but I'll weather it if you give me your word now that you'll make an honest effort to see this from my angle. Will you Sue?"

"Yes, Glyn. Of course I will."

"And, as I've said, at the end, if you still want to live alone, then I won't prevent you. On the other hand, if you decide you'd like to come back to me, I promise I'll make no unnecessary demands on you. We have one child, and I'll be content to leave it so."

"Glyn ... if, if I can't bring myself to return to you, you'll understand and forgive me, won't you?"

"Naturally." His voice had become hard.

"That doesn't sound over-convincing!" she chided him gently, then added: "Promise me that you'll try to see how I feel about all this?"

"Yes."

"Good."

"Then it's all settled?"

She nodded.

"I'll write and let you know which day to expect me. And, remember, Sue, they'll be the most important days of our lives." He stood up. "Thermos ready? I must go now."

He kissed the baby's chubby hand and gave Susan's arm a gentle squeeze.

"Goodbye, Sue."

She swallowed.

"'Bye, Glyn."

He started the engine, then leaned towards her again, his face tense and anxious.

"Oh, and Sue, you'll give me a fair chance?" She nodded.

"I will."

"Splendid. 'Bye!"

Glyn smiled and drove away. Susan saw him look in the mirror and this time he raised a hand to her before the car rounded the corner.

CHAPTER NINETEEN

Susan began to feel like a girl again. Each morning before she took Tony down to the tea-shop, she would watch for the postman. Then at last, the longed-for letter arrived. She ripped open the envelope impatiently and quickly read Glyn's untidy handwriting.

He was taking fourteen days leave, not ten, and expected to reach the village some time in the early evening on Saturday ... in four days! He told her he had wanted to make it a late Friday arrival but pressure of work obliged him to spend a few hours in the office on Saturday.

As Saturday approached, Susan decided to keep Tony up until after Glyn's arrival, as long as it was no later than seven o'clock. After all, wasn't the child the reason for her husband's visit?

On Saturday, Susan left the "Honeypot" at half-past four and collected Tony from Fiona. She took him home and gave him his tea. It was therefore a complete surprise to find Glyn on her doorstep shortly before five.

"Come in," she told him. "I didn't expect you so soon. We were coming down to the quay to surprise you. It was a special treat for Tony. I'll get you some tea."

After he had finished tea, they played with Tony until it was time for Susan to take him upstairs for a bath. Glyn remained in the lounge. Later, Susan reappeared in the doorway, her towelling apron soaked.

"Glyn," she began awkwardly, "I've tucked him in. Would you like to go up and say good night?"

"Please don't tickle or overexcite him in any way, will you, because the little rascal'll play up all evening. He's just like other children ... loves a lot of attention."

Glyn stood up.

"Takes after me, I suppose," he said and grinned wickedly. "I was a poisonous brat, you know, and you needn't start to agree with me. Oh, while I'm away, you might care to read this. Mother asked me to give it to you." He handed her a sealed envelope which Susan took, puzzled.

She could hardly believe her eyes on reading the letter's contents. In it, Beatrice and Edward begged her to forgive them for their appalling treatment of her over Tony and the cruel, unkind things they had said to her in the past.

She sat in a chair listening to Glyn talking upstairs with Tony. It must have taken Beatrice a tremendous amount of courage to write as she had done, and her heart thawed a little. If she went back to Glyn, then she too would try to help the elder Mohrs forget the past, but it was far too early to say what she was planning to do.

Five minutes later, Glyn returned, looking pleased. She put the letter back into its envelope and left it on the table. He did not ask her what it had been about.

"He's a wonderful child, Sue. You've done well." Then he sat in a chair and glanced up at her.

"Glyn, have you planned to have supper at the inn, or would you like to eat here with me?"

"With you, please. There are lots and lots of questions I want to ask about Tony, and the sort of things he does."

"Glyn, before we go any further, I want to know one thing. That awful business the other day, was it honestly nothing to do with you?"

He stared at her, his face suddenly bleak.

"Go on," he ordered harshly. "You've said so much you might as well finish."

"Well, it had crossed my mind that perhaps you had all planned it between you," she explained, unhappily.

"You accuse me of duplicity. You think the abduction was a put-up job?"

"Oh no Glyn, I'm sorry! I see I was quite wrong . . . it's just that . . ." she faltered as she went quickly to join him.

"I know exactly what you meant, my dear. You distrust everything I do. I suppose you even have suspicions concerning my visit now?

"Look at me, Sue, look hard at me! Oh, I can read your mind, my dear. You suspect me of coming here solely to get to know Tony so well that it'll make it far too difficult for you to decide once you've seen how close Tony and I become. Am I right?'' He paused, and she nodded her head almost imperceptibly.

"I swear to you, Sue, that I don't want it to happen like that! Even if I never see my son again after this fortnight, I don't want you to come back to me because you ought to for Tony's sake. I want you to come because you want to ..."

She felt a surge of excitement. Was it possible ...?

Eagerly she searched his face but he had his emotions well under control and she could read nothing at all behind that carefully veiled and inscrutable façade. She sighed.

On Monday morning, Glyn arrived with a pile of newspapers and a bulging briefcase. He grimaced.

"I hope you don't mind, Sue, but I couldn't get all my work finished before I left. If you're busy with the chores, perhaps I could sort out some of this mess in the privacy of the lounge? When you've finished, I'll take you and Tony into town for lunch."

"If you don't mind, it'd be easier to give him his lunch here. Perhaps we could go out in the car afterwards?" Susan suggested.

She experienced a strange feeling of satisfaction to work in the kitchen, knowing that Glyn was busy in the next room. It was homely and warming. Halfway through the morning she took him a cup of coffee. He was sitting in front of the table, with papers strewn all over the place and the dailies open at the commercial pages. He was completely absorbed in his work, so she put the cup at his side and turned to go. Then he looked up, peering at her through heavy-rimmed spectacles.

"How about packing a picnic tea for later?" he suggested. "I found some attractive and secluded coves on my meanderings a few weeks ago."

They drove into a small cove where they found two other cars parked. The beach was wide and with plenty of clean, yellow sand. Glyn spread the car rug for Susan and Tony, and they all sat down. It was a happy afternoon, sitting there and gazing out to sea. The breeze was still warm. although it was late in the season, and the sky was almost cloudless. Tony shuffled about on his rear, playing with handfuls of sand and a small wooden spade they had bought him.

Each morning she found herself eagerly awaiting Glyn's arrival. She became anxious if he was a few minutes late, although she took care he did not notice her concern. When he left the cottage every evening, it was at a reasonably early hour.

"Mustn't give your neighbors anything to gossip about!" he said jokingly when she tried to persuade him to stay longer. Her eyes widened in astonishment.

"Why not? You're still my husband, aren't you?"

"Am I?" he asked searchingly. "I think if I stayed too long, I might be tempted not to leave at all." He moved closer to her. "Sue ..."

She pushed him away.

"Please, Glyn, this wasn't part of the agreement."

"Now you understand why I go gack to the inn early," he said grinning. He opened the front door. "'Night, Sue."

"Good' night, Glyn." She closed the door after him, and walked slowly back into the lounge where the smell of his pipe lingered.

The days passed quickly. Glyn and Susan went for

walks and outings in his car, lazed on the beach or in the garden, and on one or two occasions they braved the cold sea for a swim.

On another occasion, Glyn absented himself to take Roger out. They drove to a hotel in town where they dined. Susan suspected that Glyn wanted to discuss her with Roger, and she was right.

Glyn came straight to the point.

"This won't take long," he began, "but I'm going to put my cards on the table. I want Sue back, although I know you love her. So, the best man wins. If she won't return to me, then I promise to provide the necessary evidence for her to divorce me, after which she'll marry you."

"You have the advantage over me, Glyn. You're already married to Sue."

Glyn shrugged.

"But she loves you, or so I have strong reason to believe ... unfortunately for me."

"I wish I had your confidence," Roger mused.

They went sailing the following week. Roger and Amanda returned to the cottage to partake of a cold supper Sue and Glyn had prepared beforehand.

"Would you like a hot drink?" Susan asked Glyn, as she shut the door behind her two friends. "I can warm the coffee again, there's still a little left."

"No thanks. I'm not staying long. I just wanted to tell you something ... for your ears alone, you might say."

"Oh?"

"Yes. I've enjoyed every moment of today, and I wanted to say a special thank you." He picked up his thick sweater from the back of the armchair, then went out into the hall.

Suddenly his arms were round her like a tight band and he was pulling her against his chest. Then he kissed her.

"Good-night, Sue," he said as she jerked away.

"Glyn! I don't know yet. That was unfair."

"Course it was!" he grinned good-naturedly back at her. "That was just to give you something to think about until we meet in the morning."

As she went to bed, she was very thoughtful. Glyn's kiss had been almost flippant. She knew what she had to do the day after tomorrow, but did he? Was he prepared to face the truth which she believed to lie within him? Even though she loved him she couldn't possibly go back to him unless he told her he also loved her.

CHAPTER TWENTY

There were only twenty-four hours left. Thinking back over the past thirteen days, Susan knew they had been a success after all. Glyn had been generous and kind to both her and Tony. It had been a pleasant change to be able to afford the more expensive foodstuffs and vary her diet. She had accepted Glyn's financial help as a matter of course and now that it was over she would have to return to careful household management.

Unless he told her he loved her . . .

Roger came to the cottage that morning, while Glyn was down in the village.

"I know Glyn isn't here," he said, coming straight to the point. "But I had to see you alone. Sue, I can't bear this suspense any more. I had to come this way to see old Mrs. Hawker, and decided to have your answer one way or the other. Please, what are you going to do?"

He looked like a small boy, standing there by the

lounge door, a hurt expression on his usually cheerful face.

Susan had to smile.

"Oh, Roger! You and Glyn are so amusing. As if having a time limit set to a problem could ever hope to bring it to a satisfactory solution! Especially where love's concerned. No, Roger, a fortnight isn't enough."

"Then ...?"

"I knew long, long ago what I wanted to do!" she declared. "The question is, does Glyn? Yes, Roger, my place is with him. How could it possibly be otherwise? It's always been Glyn," she added gently.

"I see. I'm sorry, Sue, but I'd hoped you might find it in your heart to love me instead."

She touched his arm.

"Dear Roger! I'm afraid I haven't been very fair. You see, I love my husband, and I hope and pray he still loves me. I *think* he does, but I want him to tell me so."

Outside the cottage, Glyn walked up the garden path.

"In the past week," Susan went on, "his interest in Tony has taken second place in my favor and I *know* he needs me. If only he'd find the courage to tell me in so many words!" She sighed.

Glyn quietly opened the front door and came into the hall.

"I'm glad, Sue, I hope you'll be happy," Roger replied softly.

Glyn walked towards the open lounge and paused, unnoticed, as he heard Roger say:

"You know I love you, Sue, and your happiness

comes first. Are you sure you know what you're doing?''

"Yes, Roger, I'm quite sure."

He smiled ruefully and took her hands in his, unaware of the silent onlooker standing in the shadowed hall.

"Kiss me, Sue!" he urged. Obediently she raised her face to his. At once the watcher turned and walked quickly out of the cottage, as silently as he had arrived. He went down the path and swung his step towards the village. His face was set. It was as if the bottom had fallen out of his world. Yet who was to blame? Himself, naturally, for he had known Susan had not loved him. He realized he ought to have been prepared for this to happen, but somehow he had put off thinking about it, and had just hoped ... and hoped. It was time he moved off homeward. No Susan, no Tony ... nothing but a life of agonizing loneliness ahead.

He went into the inn and asked for his bill. Then he went upstairs to pack.

Less than five minutes after Glyn had left the cottage, Roger also came out. Susan waved cheerfully to him, and then returned to wait for Glyn. He had promised to be there by ten, and he was never late.

The minutes ticked by and still he did not arrive.

What had happened? Susan wondered as the minute hand crept on and on. It was nearly a quarter to eleven.

By this time she was considerably alarmed. She decided to go down to the village and find out where he was. Tony was asleep in the pram, so she wheeled him out of the garden and along the street. She enquired for Glyn at the inn.

"Is Mr. Mohr here?" she asked anxiously.

"No, ma'am. He vacated his room less than half an hour ago."

"You mean ... he's gone?" She could not believe it. "Are you sure? Perhaps his car's still in the car park?"

The innkeeper went out to the back, and then returned almost at once, shaking his head.

"I'm sorry, Mrs. Mohr. The car isn't there either."

"Oh no!" Susan wailed. "Thank you." She ran out of the inn, looking to left and right.

Why had Glyn gone so suddenly? Where was he? Surely he couldn't have started on his journey home without coming to see her, to explain?

She wheeled the pram into the back garden of the "Honeypot".

"Look after Tony, will you, please?" she begged Amanda who came out to greet her. "I can't explain now, but I won't be very long. Glyn's taken it into his head to go off somewhere, and I must find him before he returns to town ... if he hasn't gone already."

She rushed away, heading for the cliffs. Instinct guided her feet towards that particular cliff path. It was possible she might find Glyn on the beach. He had told her how beautiful it was, and the peace it gave him. The skirt of her white jersey dress was tight, impeding her progress.

She heaved a sigh of relief when she caught sight of his car parked at the side of the lane fifty yards from the cliff edge. She ran across the turf and stood on the edge panting. Shielding her eyes against the sun she searched the long stretch of grey-gold sand beneath.

A lone figure, with head bent, was ambling along the water's edge.

"Glyn! Glyn!" she called, but the wind whipped away her voice. He did not turn.

Scrambling down the cliff path, she hurried towards him, calling out as she went. The sea murmured, growing louder as she ran nearer. The sand was wet and clinging, hampering her impatient progress. She stopped, tugged off her sandals and carried them. The wet sand tickled her bare toes, but she did not care.

"Glyn, wait!" she shouted. This time he heard her. He stopped and looked around. Gasping for breath she rushed up to him and stood before him, her chest heaving.

"Oh, Glyn, why did you give me such a beastly fright? I thought you'd gone without saying good-bye."

"No, Sue. I was coming to see you, but I hadn't been able to find the courage. I needed time to think so I came down here to work out what I had to say to you before we parted."

"Then you're really going home to the city?"

"Yes."

"Why?"

"Sue, let me explain. I badly want my son, but I'm not selfish enough to take him away from you. It'd be a wicked, cruel deed. You want Roger ..."

"What makes you think that?" she interrupted.

"I saw you both earlier on."

Susan frowned.

"Saw us? What are you talking about? And what makes you think it's Roger I want? Have you gone out of your mind?"

"There's no need to lie, just to be kind," he said gently. "I saw you both, through the open lounge door. I came into the cottage ... perhaps you didn't hear me ... and you were talking. I shouldn't have listened, but somehow I couldn't help overhearing. Then I saw you kissing."

Realization dawned.

"Oh!" she sighed, relieved. "Is that all? Now I understand." She caught hold of his elbows and shook him, her smile impish. "You didn't stay very long, did you?"

"Of course not! One quick glance told me all I needed to know."

"Did it, indeed! Then perhaps I'd better refresh your memory. This is how I was kissing Roger." She pulled his head down to hers and gave him a demure kiss on the mouth. Then she released him, and her eyes sparkled. "Yet this is different," she went on, her face suddenly solemn. "*This* is the way I might have kissed him had he been the man I loved." She flung her arms tightly around his neck, pressed one hand hard against the back of his head and strained upwards. Her parted lips then met his with an ardency that amazed and thrilled him. She arched her body against his and began to tremble.

"Oh, you fool, you fool!" she moaned. "Can't you understand?" He tasted the salt tears welling out from under her closed eyelids. Then she flung herself away from him.

"Show me, Glyn, show me you love me! Kiss me, oh kiss me!" she begged.

With an inarticulate cry, he pulled her back into his arms and brought his mouth down on hers so roughly that she felt bruised and hurt, but did not mind. He pressed himself against her, then buried his face in her neck while she clung wildly to him, weeping with joy.

"Sue, my darling Sue! I've been so very, very stupid!"

"I know, my love, but I haven't helped you, have I?"

"I wanted to throw myself at your feet, begging you to love me, but I was afraid. Afraid of being hurt and spurned as you often did in the past."

"Sh! That was over long ago," she whispered against his searching mouth.

Time seemed endless as they stood in each other's arms, with the sea murmuring and fussing about their feet, soaking Glyn's town shoes. At long last they released each other, smiling tremulously. Then he took out a handkerchief and wiped the tears from Susan's cheeks.

"Don't cry, darling. The time for sorrow's past now."

She clung to his waist and they stood looking out to sea, where the midday sun sparkled on the wide waters. His lips caressed her neck as he murmured:

"I must know one thing! Tell me now, and I'll never again refer to it. Tony ... how and when did it happen?"

Without embarrassment Susan answered, while he watched her thoughtfully. When she had finished he smiled and looked relieved.

"Now I'm content. I know the whole truth. It's been worrying me for so long ... even before I knew about Tony. Until I saw him I couldn't believe it had been true. You see, Sue, once I began to get better, I kept remembering little things here and there. That fateful evening was like a jigsaw with many missing pieces. I knew we'd quarrelled, that was confirmed by my friends. Yet I had strange memories ... fantasies, if you like ... of the events in the garden. At first I dismissed it as part of the nightmare caused by a cracked skull. Then I met you again ... with Tony .. and knew it must have been true after all. Then the jigsaw began to fit together perfectly, except for one small piece. My first recollection after the accident was a feeling of tremendous exultation ... I was glad about something, but didn't know what. Later, I decided it must be because I was glad our marriage was over. Then ... I saw you, and Tony ...

"You see, I couldn't believe you'd welcomed me that night. I thought it must have been a figment of my imagination, wishful thinking, if you like. Now that you've told me yourself, I know I wasn't mistaken. Seeing you with Roger I was hurt, yet I wanted you to be happy even if it meant the end of all my dreams."

Susan kissed him again.

"I'm very fond of him, but he knew long ago that I wasn't the woman for him. I told him he ought to love Amanda. Glyn, you're the man I need and love."

"And it's taken us almost two years to find out!"

"Glyn, you don't have to go back today, do you?"

He smiled at her.

"Nothing could drag me away from you now, my darling. To hell with the work for another week. I'll ring them and say I'm ill, or something equally untrue. Terrible disease is love; all the worse when it comes late in life, as someone once said.''

"Glyn, what are we going to do about the future? I love it here, but I want to be with you."

"You've still part of your lease to run, haven't you? Good. Then we'll live in my ... I mean, our ... new house during the week and drive down here every weekend. Then we'll think about some different job."

"Oh no!" she began to protest.

"Don't worry, it's a question that's been given a great deal of thought for quite some time. I'm not particularly happy working for my father. I've always wanted to try my hand at something else. I'd like to live away from the big cities ... in a place like this, perhaps, and travel a few miles to my job every day."

"Oh, darling, if only you could!" Susan sighed and snuggled into Glyn's side. "We'd be so happy here." He grinned down at her.

"We can discuss all this later. In the meantime, and especially for the benefit of anyone up there on the cliff top, I'm going to kiss you again. I've got a lot of time to make up, and don't think you're going to find it easy to wriggle out of it!"

"Who said I'd want to!" she murmured, screwing her head around to look back at the land, but there was not a soul in sight. They were quite alone, with only the sea and the sky for company. She turned towards Glyn. He cupped her face in one hand and his smile was gentle. She touched his greying hair and murmured:

"To think you once terrified me!"

"I was selfish and thoughtless. You were right to

spurn me. I promise you, darling, that from now on you'll find me the most loving and gentle of husbands.''

"But still the master of the house!" she urged anxiously.

"Very much the master! That's one post I refuse to relinquish to you, my girl.'' He pulled her to him, his mouth touching her cheek and his hand caressing her neck.

"I love you, Sue," he whispered.

"I love you, Glyn," she managed to reply before their mouths met.